Cinch Your Saddle

MEGAN MICHAELS

Cover Design by Rachel A Olson
(www.nosweatgraphics.weebly.com)

This book is a work of fiction. The characters, incidents and
dialogues are products of the author's imagination and as such,
any similarity to existing persons, places or events must be
considered purely coincidental.

This book contains content that is not suitable for readers aged
17 and under.

For mature readers only.

Published in the United States of America.

ISBN: 1517276594
ISBN-13: 978-1517276591

First Print Edition: September 2015

By Megan Michaels

The Service & Submission Series:

Finding Submission

Mastering Inga

The Widow Wagon Series:

Book One: Second Chances

Book Two: More Than She Bargained For

Book Three: Cinch Your Saddle

Published By Stormy Night Publications

What Naughty Little Girls Get

The Little Princess Cruise

PROLOGUE

She stood quietly in the corner, facing the seam in the tent. It was as close to a corner as they could find on the Oregon Trail. When he'd whispered to her that they "needed to have a discussion" and told her to stand in the corner waiting, her eyes had widened, her throat working to swallow. "But why? What did I do?"

"Corner. Now." Angus had pointed toward their little tent, watching her dash in that direction. He never viewed himself as someone who would be cruel — and he wasn't — but he knew the anticipation of a spanking excited her, sending her pussy to throbbing, the pulsing muscles working up her natural essence, coating her to excess. By the time he'd made it to the tent and slid his fingers through those puffy lips, she'd be slick and ready. He'd pull away from her warm, moist quim, her spicy sent filling the air. And while she watched with a little fear and trepidation in her eyes, he'd insert his sticky fingers into his mouth, tasting her sweetness, sucking loudly as that pink blush rose from her neck to her cheekbones.

Yes, the benefits of corner time were not to be denied. Clara always responded sexually to it, in spite of her nerves being on edge. He'd given her another couple minutes before he rescued her.

He walked around the site, checking on the women, making sure they were settling in for the night. As wagon master for the Widow Wagon, he'd taken on the responsibility of making sure the women were safe and delivered to their new husbands. As a widower himself, he knew the loneliness and heartache of losing a spouse — and he also knew the joy in finding someone who fit you like a glove. He went to the wagon to be sure that Nelly and Rose were sleeping. Clara's girls were sweet and well-behaved, and he'd grown to love them while on this journey West. He spotted Sam, his assistant and cook while on this trip, saluting him as he walked by. More than a mere cook though, Sam, armed with his rifle, currently rested near the women, keeping watch for any danger during the night.

Except for the occasional cricket, a distant wolf howling, or the pop of dry wood in the fire, his spurs were the only sound on this quiet night. There wasn't a cloud in the sky, and out on the plains like this, the stars were out by the thousands. He swore when his life settled and he had a house for his family in Missouri, he'd take time to sleep out under the stars in memory of the days on the trail. He'd never grow tired of lying under the stars.

He pulled back the flap on the tent, the amber glow flickering as the candlelight danced in the breeze. She stood obediently in the corner — naked, just as he required. He didn't need to say it anymore; she knew what he liked and what was expected. He loved that his hands could span the small waist above her beautiful, broad hips. Her plump, white buttocks were firm, but had just enough softness that they wobbled when spanked. He loved squeezing and grabbing that ass, pulling her hips up to his hard cock. He'd never tire of this woman. Ever.

She stole a glance over her shoulder in his direction, and he barked at her, "Eyes forward until I say otherwise."

Her head snapped back, her feet shuffling, her thighs

rubbing together. He smiled, knowing her clit must be throbbing by now, that little rub of the thighs likely giving it a bit of relief — for a few seconds anyway. As suspected, her time in the corner had primed her for what he had planned. He folded a blanket in front of the chair he'd placed at a safe distance from the table. Everything seemed to be in place.

He sat down, rolling up the sleeves of his white work shirt. "Clara, come here."

She pivoted but halted for just a moment, not taking her eyes off the sight of his hands working on the sleeves. Nibbling on her lower lip, she finally stood in front of him, uncertain what to do with her hands, obviously struggling to keep them away from her quim. She knew covering herself was a no-no in his book.

"Hands on your head."

She obediently laced her fingers behind her head, the act alone causing her to stand straighter, her chest out. The position threw her breasts into even greater prominence, placed perfectly for his mouth. He leaned forward, squeezing and plumping the one, while pulling on the nipple of the other, capturing it between his lips, suckling until her gasp above him forced his eyes open. She stared intently, her thighs trembling. He abandoned her breast, moving his hand down to cup her sex. The damp curls of her sex left a wet sticky trail on his hand as he stroked her, grinding his upper palm on her clit, in conjunction with sucking her nipple painfully hard.

"Oh, Angus!" Her head lolled back, her mouth opening.

"That's my girl," he cooed. Angus moved his hand over her sex, letting his middle finger slide between her slick lips, tapping her clit. Her hips thrust while he let her breast slip out of his mouth but not before he teased the tip, scissoring it with his front teeth. She gasped again when he slid a finger along her silky skin, easing two fingers into her, pumping her quim. He danced the tip of his thumb on her clit, reaching around with his other hand to cup her ass, running his finger between her adorable cheeks. He stuck a finger into her back hole, and she stiffened, shouting with her release, the tight muscles constricting around him, her release sending a flood of nectar sliding down his hand to collect upon his palm. Her little puckered hole tightened on his finger, both holes milking him.

He wondered if he'd be able to hold his own release back, watching her fly apart, her body quaking with the residual tremors. His cock felt strangled under the restraint of his clothing.

During her fall over the cliff, her hands had come loose from her head and she had clawed him, his shoulders screaming in pain as the blood soaked into his shirt. That would be a stain he'd order her to leave alone though. It would be a badge of honor in his book, a memento of this night.

He released his fingers from her body, wiping them on her buttocks, her sigh at the loss making him smile. "Lie down on this blanket, girl. On your back."

She blinked at him. "I'm not getting spanked?"

"No. I just wanted you to be ready and primed, and standing in the corner does that for you." He winked at her.

She frowned at him. "Angus! I was worried."

"Well, I'm always happy to oblige. If you really want one, or you keep up with this little attitude you're working up to, I can always give you a good spanking instead."

"N-no, that's okay. I'm all right, really."

She brightened, giving him a sweet smile as she got on her hands and knees, then laid down on her back, looking up at him expectantly. He leaned forward, pulling her hair up off her shoulders, fanning it across the blanket.

"Arms above your head. Close your eyes." The pulse in her neck quickened. "You're safe, Clara. I'm not going to let anything happen to you."

He picked up a lit long, white tapered candle in each hand, the paraffin wax had pooled at the top. He kept the candles three to four feet above her body, dribbling the wax slowly onto her nipples. Gasping, her eyes fluttered open, her gaze locking upon him. He smiled, reassuring her — he hoped.

Clara closed her eyes.

Good girl.

He circled her left breast first, random drips of hot wax dotting her nipple and areola, her belly trembling. Then he went to the right, circling that nipple, making a similar pattern. He let the wax pool on the candles, while he blew softly on the warm liquid, watching the skin goose bump on each of her breasts. Tilting the candles close together, the flames kissed the outer edge, wax flowing downward in gentle rivulets from her sternum to her navel.

The muscles of her thighs stiffened, her hips moving just a fraction of an inch. He pulled up the candles. "You can move, darlin'. Is it feeling good?"

"Yes, Sir." She arched her back, feet flat on the bed, pulling her knees up, her pelvis swiveling. Then she relaxed, widening her legs, her pussy clearly visible through the thin veil of pubic hair. He placed the candles back into their stands, allowing his finger the freedom to stray. His hand drew lazy circles on her inner hip, her body writhing under the attention.

"Oh, God!" She lifted her bottom off the blanket, unable to keep still under his teasing fingers. He rubbed just above her pussy, twirling the curls under his fingers, brushing over her labia but not pressing or entering.

She tried pushing him to give her sexual pleasure.

"Clara, keep your fingers away!"

He furrowed his eyebrows at her when she opened her lids. She quickly shuttered them again, returning her hands to her head.

"You know better than that, bad girl. I control what happens, and when it happens."

MEGAN MICHAELS

To prove his point, he barely stroked her, lightly brushing the little brown tuft of hair, tapping her clit once before he abandoned her.

Her whine made him chuckle, and she squeezed her thighs together tightly, one of her subtle methods of self-gratification.

He grasped the candles again; the wax had pooled nicely. He let the hot liquid drip slowly down each hip, being careful not to get it anywhere near her pubic hair or sex. He let it kiss a trail up her belly to her sternum again, the warm fluid melting the partially-cooled wax beneath it.

Clara gasped in response to the warm wax hitting the soft skin on her belly. Tilting the candles together again, the hiss of the flame dancing in the wax and the smell of burning candles filled the air. As the wax dripped in a steady stream onto her body, he circled each areola, focusing on the nipple itself this time, the skin bumping and puckering tightly under the attention. Turning his attention to the right one, he gave the same treatment to the other soft globe, leaving the areola buried beneath the sticky wax. "You can move, baby. Just keep your hands above your head."

Her petulant whine in response never failed to make him grin.

Adorable.

He returned the candles to their stands, divesting himself of his clothes. At the sound of the buckle being undone, her eyes opened, staring at him as he quickly pulled the leather free of the loops of his pants. He enjoyed the way she shivered at the *whap, whap, whap* sound as the tip of the thick belt slapped through them.

He swore his cock groaned when he let it free from the restraints of his clothing. He gripped the silky, hot length, stroking himself, watching her lick her lips reflexively, her hips unable to lie still. He hovered over her body, resting on the cradle of her hips, both hands grabbing onto her breasts, plumping them, the wax melting under his hot

6

caress, thumbing the erect nipples, peeling the wax off under his rough touch. Lifting his hips, his forearms braced to either side of her, he positioned his penis to penetrate her, thrusting deep. Enveloping her mouth under his, she moaned into his mouth, her pussy constricting upon his hot, turgid member, a strangled groan bubbling up from his chest in response.

He ground his hips into her pelvis, pistoning his cock into her hot, moist cunt. She groaned, tilting her head back, exposing her slender throat, her sighs and moans coming faster and louder. Angus felt that familiar tingle in the base of his spine compelling him to thrust into her hard, shouting his release shortly after her scream, the vice-like grip of her sex throwing him over the edge. Their hips continued to thrust and squeeze, milking every drop of cum from each other. They lay in that beautiful place between ecstasy and reality, where only the pulsing of their sex and their gasps for air mattered.

"Jesus, girl." His semi-erect penis slipped from between her swollen labia as he rolled onto his side next to her. "Looks like we succeeded in getting most of the wax off of you — and onto me." He pulled at the hardened white pieces now embedded in his chest hair.

Clara giggled, covering her mouth as if she could hide her laughter from him. "It looks good on your breasts too."

"Bad girl," he said, grinning. Sitting, he began to pull wax out of his chest hair, dropping it into a pile on the blanket. "Let's clean up and get to bed. Wagon leaves early in the morning."

CHAPTER ONE

Two weeks earlier

Angus swore there was nothing more beautiful than the Wyoming sky. Blue as one of those small marbles he had in the bag in his pocket. Not a cloud in the sky, and in the distance the Granite Mountains could be seen. It wouldn't be long before they arrived in Independence Rock, another drop-off. Clara would be meeting her new husband. Angus sighed, knowing he'd miss Clara and the kids.

It had been a long time since he'd been able to play with children, enjoying their laughter and their antics. He chuckled to himself — kids brought an enjoyment to life that some didn't know. Others, like himself, knew the joy and chaos that children brought to a home, and he knew the void and heartbreaking pain of their loss. He swiped at the tears that sprung up unbidden — again.

This past winter marked three years since his wife and little girls had succumbed to influenza. He'd never understand why God hadn't taken him too; he'd cared for and nursed them all for weeks. His wife's name had been Rose, just like Clara's youngest. She'd turned twenty seven the year she'd given up the ghost. Their girls were five and seven — Katherine and Priscilla. He'd nicknamed them Kat and Prissy. Rose never cared for their nicknames, instead wanting them to sound like elegant ladies of society. Angus told her that there'd be time enough for that...

Angus spent hours on the floor with them in the evening. Playing marbles, tickling, letting them jump on him and ride him like a horse — he missed the laughter and mayhem a busy house with young children brought. His wife some days had been appalled that he roughhoused with them "like boys —they're girls Angus, not roughneck boys!"

He'd done his best to save them, and the doctor had told him so too. He'd bathed them, sat up all night putting cold compresses on their heads, serving them broth. He'd even gone to town to get them the latest remedies. Rose had been afraid that he'd catch it, and told him repeatedly to put a handkerchief over his face.

"Angus, just worry about the girls. I'm fine. I don't need you fussin' over me like a mother hen." She'd scowl at him, but was so weak near the end that she couldn't so much as lift her head from her pillow.

"Don't you bark out orders at me, girl. I do what I want and you know that. You need to get well." Then he'd put a compress on her head, gently kissing her lips. "What would I do without you? Promise me you'll get better."

"I'm doin' my best, Angus. How's Kat and Prissy?" At that thought, she'd tried to rise up to see them across the room.

Angus had pulled the mattresses into the main room of the house so that he could take care of all of them and watch them closely at the same time. He'd slept — when he could — in the rocking chair by the fire.

"They're doin' fine. You go back to sleep. You don't wanna disturb them, do ya?" He'd gently pushed her back onto her pillow then, tucking the warm quilt around her

9

neck to keep away the chill of the Missouri January.

"No, I don't want to wake them. Keep them cool. Did you get any medicine from the Doc?" Her eyes were glassy, her cheeks pink with the fever he couldn't keep down.

"Yes. Doc gave me medicine for both you and the kids. Don't you remember takin' it?" He tried not to alarm her, but if she'd forgotten, it meant her fever and the influenza had taken hold harder than he'd anticipated.

Her eyebrows had knit in confusion. "No. You gave me medicine?"

He tried to sound casual, seeing concern in her eyes. "Just a couple times in the middle of the night," he lied. "That's probably why you don't remember. Just go to sleep. I'll give you more when it's time. I need to check on the girls." He kissed her forehead, then rose wearily from the bed to go see his girls.

His wife would never wake again.

She'd been the first to go. After discovering she'd died, he'd crawled into bed with her and wept over her lifeless body. He'd covered her with the blue and yellow patchwork quilt her mother had made them for their wedding. It was funny the things one thought at moments like those. Her mother had no idea years ago that the very quilt she made for their wedding bed would also be the quilt used to cover her lifeless, cold daughter before she'd been buried under the brown Missouri dirt. He stayed with Rose until he had to check on the girls, replacing cloths, giving medicine, and feeding them both broth.

He slept on the end of the girls' bed, taking turns caring for each of them. Kat and Prissy had hair so blonde it was white, their piercing blue eyes as glassy as the marbles they played with at night. Their lips were cherry red with fever, and he did his best to keep them drinking water. But it had been difficult when they were so listless that the water dribbled out of the corner of their mouths. He'd finally taken to serving water to them with a spoon.

He knew the night that Prissy died that he'd lost the battle for both of his daughters. They hardly coughed anymore. But their lungs, full of infection, rattled and wheezed, their little bodies struggling for air, even as they appeared calm and almost...peaceful. He'd given them more broth, hoping to clear up their lungs. The Doc had said it would help. But when Prissy started to have the fits, tremors ravaging her for minutes on end, he knew the fever had won.

He'd be losing his daughter that night.

Exhaustion had taken over and he'd collapsed at some point at the end of the bed, waking much later, startled to see sunlight shining through the little kitchen window in the main room. He had leapt out of bed, touching Prissy's face. *Cold and gray.* She was gone.

He'd slept, and his baby girl had died.

Common sense told him that it had nothing to do with him falling asleep, but he worried that she'd died alone. Did she cry out for him? No. He would've woken up if she had. Right? Did she reach out looking for his arms to hold her as she left this world? No, he would have felt the movement in the bed. She had been listless all day. She more than likely just drifted off, carried quietly by the angels out of this world.

He'd scooped up his baby girl, her arms falling, dangling over his own. Tucking her nightie over her legs, he'd sat by the fire — to keep her warm. It didn't make sense. He knew she wasn't cold — but she felt cold. His paternal instincts were impossible to fight; part of him still yearned to keep her warm, comfortable, and safe. Then he'd dropped his face against her clammy neck and wept. He'd miss cuddling with his baby Prissy. She'd been the one that sat on his lap or tucked herself under his arm in bed on those cold, lazy Sunday mornings. She loved laying on his chest, hugging his neck. Those little arms wouldn't wrap around him ever again. He didn't know how long he'd sat there holding her. But when the time came to give

Kat her medicine, he'd gently placed Prissy in the bed, tucking the quilt around her just as he had for her mother.

When he'd rounded the bed, his lively and full of mischief Kat seemed as listless as her sister had been the day before. With a low whine from deep within, he dropped his head to her small, slight chest and just wept. He'd never understood why God didn't hear his wails and cries. He remembered the preacher saying that God saved his tears in Heaven. If He would go to the trouble to save them, why couldn't He just prevent the tears? It seemed like Angus had been abandoned.

He had wiped the tears away, giving Kat her medicine, wiping her brow, and ladling her the same broth he'd given Prissy. Surely God would let Kat live. He wouldn't let Angus be totally alone — lost. Angus diligently cared for Kat, doing everything he knew to make her well.

But when nightfall came around and Kat had started to have the fits too, he knew he'd lost this battle as well. He'd held her body, waiting for the fits to end and wailed loudly, begging God to take his life instead. But his prayers obviously didn't reach Heaven.

Kat had died a few hours later.

Angus had held her in his arms in front of the fire, remembering the antics and fun he'd had with his Kat. From the time she could walk, she climbed and ran almost nonstop. She wasn't dainty or delicate as Prissy had been. His Kat had been a tomboy. She loved to fish and catch frogs at the pond. She'd been the boy he hadn't been graced with. He'd find her climbing trees and sitting in the loft of the barn. If mischief didn't find her, she found it. She'd been on the receiving end of her parents' discipline many a day, and although he wouldn't let her know it, he loved that about her. She had a zest and zeal for life. He always believed she'd do something important someday. It looked like he'd been wrong. He'd laid his lifeless daughter onto the bed next to her sister, covering her too.

Sitting in his chair by the fireplace, he stared at what

used to be his family. He would need to call the doctor and let him know and receive death certificates for all of them. Writing to Rose's family would be a very difficult task--one he dreaded. How would he tell them that their daughter— their only daughter had died in Missouri. Then burying them would be the next task. He'd bury them under the willow tree by the pond, putting a fence around it. He rocked, and stared, and thought. Rose died on a Sunday, Prissy on Monday, and Kat on Tuesday — the same day his own life had ended.

When he'd finally gotten up and saddled his horse for town, he'd headed for Doc's office first. Upon his arrival, he'd been told that it was Saturday. *Saturday!* He had sat on the chair in his house for four days. Doc said he'd gone into shock, and he'd given him some medicine to combat it before insisting he come to Mabel's for some dinner.

The town had rallied around him after his tragic loss. Friends had coordinated making the caskets. They had dug the graves and helped him bury his family. The mason in town made him some simple stones with their names, dates of birth, and dates of death. He visited that little cemetery by the pond almost every day. He'd fish and remember the days of laughing with Kat and walking home with a line full of five-inch fish. His girls had bragged about those fish as if they were whales.

The women in town had cooked meals for him. He didn't have to ask or beg either. Rather, he'd come home and find a meal sitting by the fire, all ready for him. He'd helped out as a marshal in Independence for years, and when Charles had mentioned to him he'd be starting a mail order Widow Wagon service for the Oregon Trail, Angus knew it would be the right job for him. It would keep him away from home — which wasn't a home anymore. It was a house, nothing more. He'd get to help lonely, needy women to start over again. And in the process, he'd get to enjoy the country. It had been a perfect fit.

Starting over again after losing them was hard, a

daunting task he didn't even know how to start. But a friend had said to him one day, "Angus, you gotta cinch your saddle and start over. You can't mope in that house every day. It's time." He'd been right.

Today, driving the wagon to Independence Rock, Wyoming, he looked at the landscape around him, and decided that he might not be as happy as he had been. Life had turned out pretty well for him, all things considered. He liked being the wagon master for the Widow Wagon. And except for the occasional woman like Daisy — who did nothing but rile up the other women — he really enjoyed the job.

He hated having to discipline the women, but he knew from hard experience that they could cause quite a ruckus if he didn't keep them in line. This particular Widow Wagon had been a challenge; the women were an interesting mix and every single one of them was independent, strong-willed, and sassy as hell. He still felt bad about having to switch Clara the week before, but she and Daisy hadn't given him any choice. He'd found the grown women rolling around on the ground, pulling each other's hair — and then Clara had decided to switch Daisy after he'd specifically warned her not to.

He'd miss Clara and her girls though. He played with them every night and it reminded him of his own girls. They were good girls and fun. But his job was to deliver women to their future husbands at designated stops on the Oregon Trail. Today, he'd be delivering Clara, and her adorable daughters Rose, and Nelly.

The wagon pulled up in front of the station stop in Independence Rock, Wyoming. Twisting in the wind, the sign for the station dangled by one corner from the single remaining chain suspending it. In the distance, a small creek could be seen, which would make a good stop for the wagon for the night. Angus looked at the station stop, the weather worn clapboards had faded into a drab gray from the harsh Wyoming elements. "Clara, girls! C'mon out. It's time to meet your new husband and pa."

He jumped down from the wagon bench and Clara came from the back of the wagon with the girls. He wrapped his large hands around each girls' slight shoulders, walking them up to the station window. "Hey Dusty, we're here to meet a gentleman by the name of Eugene Wilson, for a Clara Pickett."

Dusty grabbed his book and flipped through the pages. "I thought so. The name was familiar to me when ya said it." He closed the book with a finality that Angus didn't like. "Eugene came here yesterday and a mail-order bride had been left standing here, stranded. He said he'd take her. They done got married at the chapel up the road, then they left town."

"He left with another *woman*?" Angus couldn't keep the incredulity from his voice.

"Yep, that's what I said. He told her that he'd take her and said something about 'not wanting young'uns anyway' and he left to marry her." Dusty shrugged at them. "Sorry. Is there anything else I can do for you?"

"No. What you did has been fine. Good day."

Angus turned to Clara, who had tears streaming down her face as she peered up at him. "Now, I'm alone. What am I going to do?"

"You ain't going to do anything. You'll stay with the Widow Wagon, and I'll take care of you. We'll figure something out. You've lost one husband and now this — but it doesn't mean you give up. You just take a deep breath, cinch your saddle, and move forward. One foot in front of the other. It's all ya can do some days. One step at a time."

He pulled his handkerchief from his pocket, wiping her eyes probably a little too roughly. And then, turning to the girls, said, "Who wants a few candy sticks from the mercantile? And maybe we'll get some ice cream after dinner too."

"Angus!" Clara shouted. "It's too much. You'll spoil

them."

"There's no such thing, girl. Women are made for spoilin'. When given the chance, you let people know you care for them. If you behave, I may just spoil you too." He chucked her under the chin, winking at her. "C'mon Clara, let's get you a grape candy stick too!"

She laughed even as she wiped at her tears, then linked her hand into the crook of his waiting elbow.

CHAPTER TWO

Clara plodded behind the wagon with the other women, the dust floating through the air as they traveled past several wooden-framed stores and saloons in the center of town. Off in the distance, she saw all the other covered wagons in the area, campfires dotting the landscape among the children running and playing, the women cooking the dinner meals. The women of the Widow Wagon had been kind to her and said things that would comfort her. "He wasn't any good if he could just leave you." Or they said, "What kind of man does that? You wouldn't want him if he could leave a woman with two girls alone." And they were right, of course. But it made no sense. She still felt jilted, the sting of rejection. He'd never even met her! He just decided to take on a new woman, no waiting to see, no pause to think it over first. He simply walked up to this woman and said he'd take her — marry her — versus the completely different stranger he'd ordered be brought to him via the Widow Wagon. Well, if he didn't want any young'uns, she'd be better off without him anyway.

Or would she?

She'd have to go all the way to the Oregon Territory

now, and then return alone with Angus to Independence, Missouri. The thought of it made her feel sick to her stomach. Thousands of miles of walking, not to mention the risk of losing her girls to illness or the elements.

At the station, when Eugene had never shown up, Angus had said, "I'll take care of you. We'll figure something out." What had he meant by that? He'd been kind and taken care of her and the girls — well, in reality, he took care of all the women on the Widow Wagon. But he did seem to take particular interest in her and the girls. And they enjoyed him too.

They pulled up to the other wagons in a haphazard jumble spread across the countryside, and Angus brought the oxen and horses to the creek to drink. Clara and Lizzie pulled out the cooking supplies and utensils from the wagon, setting up the fire and cooking pot. Sam took over at that point, starting the evening meal, while the women kept the kids occupied with some games.

Angus walked up to her and the girls. "You ready to go to dinner, girl?"

"Angus, we can have dinner with the rest of the women. There isn't any need to spend money on a dinner." It seemed frivolous and silly, and the last thing she needed was one of the women from the wagon deciding he favored her and the girls.

"It ain't up for discussion, girl. I told ya that I was bringing you and the girls to eat, and I keep my promises. I'm not going to hear another argument from you. You hear?" He leveled her with a steely gaze, his jaw clenched. It seemed important to him, and Lord knew she didn't want to tangle with him again.

"I hear. Thank you, Angus." She turned to the girls. "Thank Mister Angus for bringing us to eat — and both of you better mind your manners in there."

By that point, both of the girls were skipping instead of walking, unable to contain their excitement. They'd never eaten in a restaurant before. "Thank you, Mister Angus," they shouted in unison.

Nelly, the oldest of Clara's girls, smiled at both of them. "We'll be on our best behavior, Ma. Promise."

"See Miss Clara, they're good girls. They wouldn't think of misbehavin'. I reckon they don't even know *how* to misbehave."

He winked her way, chuckling. But when she looked at her girls they were beaming. He made them feel so grown up, and just his belief that they'd behave made their little chests puff in pride.

And to her delight, they acted like little ladies, each of them eating quietly, with their mouths closed, napkins on their laps. But when Angus asked the server to bring everyone a bowl of ice cream, they both shrieked, clapping their hands until they looked her way and saw the warning glare she shot them. Immediately, they stopped and folded their hands in their laps.

"Now, why did you have to go and do that, Miss Clara? They were just excited about ice cream. As adults, if we got that excited about ice cream, we'd find ourselves a much happier lot."

"That doesn't mean you lose your manners in the process, Mr. Angus." She glared at him too. Who did he think he was telling her how to raise her girls?

He raised his eyebrows at her, turning in his chair to look at her straight on. "I didn't say nothing about losing your manners. They were excited. People have no problem with children being happy — except their ma, apparently. And don't you decide to give me attitude, Missy."

"I wouldn't think of giving you attitude." She smiled at him coquettishly. She had been watching him closely during the journey, and had concluded he was more bark than bite. Even so, if pushed, his bite *was* serious indeed. The still-fading marks on her own backside could attest to that.

He tried to hide a smirk, but Clara saw it. He was a good man, and probably had been a good husband. He'd mentioned one night that he'd lost his wife and two little girls to influenza. It'd been hard enough to lose her own husband to dropsy. The doc said his heart had never been good, and after enduring weakness and illness for a couple years, her husband had finally succumbed. But she didn't even want to think about losing her girls too. How did he get up and start his life again? How did he move forward?

He'd said he'd cinched his saddle. And that's just what she'd do too.

* * *

After their dinner, Clara tucked the quilts around her girls, kissing their foreheads before climbing out of the wagon. The sky had darkened into night with faint streaks of pink just at the horizon. She stretched out her sleeping bag near the fire, trying to keep hers distant from the others yet still close to the fire. She knew she'd be fighting tears tonight, and she wanted to face them without an audience.

Relief flooded through her at the knowledge that her girls were safe in the wagon, and wouldn't hear her sniffling, wondering if they should be concerned or afraid. Angus insisted from day one that the girls were to sleep in the wagon at night. He said the night air wouldn't be good for them, and he'd feel better having them safe in the wagon. Clara found Angus interesting. He had a rough and tough exterior, but inside he was very gentle and kind. Her girls adored him, and she had no doubt that they'd miss him when they departed.

Departed to where?

Her life seemed so uncertain now. One husband dead, the other would-be-husband left with another woman before he'd even met Clara. And now, she was alone with two little girls in the middle of Wyoming, trying to decide if she would go back to Indiana, or make her home in Missouri. It all felt so overwhelming. The tears stung and burned behind her eyes and though she fought it, they fell regardless. She pulled her sleeping bag over her head, trying to hide from the others.

The past year had been so difficult. She'd lived through so many changes since Matt died. That damn rusty nail in the barn. She knew the day he came in with his foot bleeding that it would be trouble. They'd done home remedies for it, but no matter what they did, it festered up. She'd made several poultices for it, but it just kept getting worse and worse until that day he woke up with a fever, his back, neck, and jaw constricted. He couldn't move out of the bed, turn his head, or talk. *Lockjaw.*

Two days later he started having fits from the fever, his body spasming and then the dropsy took him. Her girls had missed him so much. They still did. If Eugene wasn't for them, it was better to have him leave now than to break their hearts again. They couldn't mourn over someone they'd never met. If anything, they seemed happier that they weren't going to say goodbye to Angus. They had truly fallen in love with him; he'd become their favorite playmate — a playmate with rules and boundaries. He supported Clara every step of the way and he never, *ever* undermined her authority. She appreciated that about him.

Angus steadfastly supported rules and respected the boundaries. He'd told her not to fight with Daisy, specifically warning her not to take a switch to the woman if she came after Rose and Nelly. But Clara's temper took over, and she had switched Daisy's bare backside. As a result, Angus had done the same to her in return. She still flushed with embarrassment thinking of him seeing her bare bottom.

"Hey, girl. Are ya okay?" Angus put a hand on her shoulder and Clara jumped, almost shouting in alarm.

"Jesus, Angus, you scared the living hell out of me!" She rolled onto her back, scowling at him. You'd think a man would know not to startle a woman in the night.

"Easy. I just wanted to check on ya. Make sure you were okay after the events of the day today." He paused, averting his eyes, looking almost...uncomfortable. She wondered if he wasn't exactly sure how to be tender. Or perhaps he did, but was wary of showing it? Either way, he seemed uncertain what to do now that she'd yelled at him.

"Before we wake everyone up, come on over to my tent and we can talk." He stood up from his squatting position, his hand outstretched toward her.

She looked quickly over her shoulder at the other women to ascertain if any of them would notice them leaving. "Angus...I'm not sure this is proper. What will the women say if they see us going to your tent?"

"I don't really care what the women say. Why do you?" He stopped walking to look her in the face.

"Well. I don't know." Clara shrugged, feeling embarrassed to admit it to him. "I guess I do because women talk and they gossip about such things. I've had a bad enough week — hell, a bad enough *year* — that I don't need a bunch of women gossiping about me."

He grabbed her hand and said, "There ain't nothing to gossip about. We're talking. That's it." He opened the flap on the tent, revealing a little table inside, the space lit by two candles and a small oil lantern. There was a single wooden spindle chair and a cot for sleeping. He pointed to the chair. "Sit."

She pushed her hair behind her ear, smiling at him and sitting uncomfortably on the chair with her back straight, hands folded in her lap. "Am I in trouble?"

"You weren't — at first. But after the swearing outburst you just had, I should give you a couple hard swats to mind your language. I'm sure you were trained better than that. I'm bettin' that you weren't allowed to use such language when you was married, right?"

She swallowed. His assumption about language was correct. Matt would've soaped her mouth or paddled her for sure. He wanted the girls raised by a quiet, proper mother. In his absence, she'd become a little lackadaisical about her language when she became upset. Knowing it wasn't a good example to the girls, she told them to 'do as she said, not as she did.'

"Maybe you deserve a few swats if you're going to be defiant and not answer me." Angus stepped in front of her, thumbs hooked in his belt. Her eyes were level with those rough hands, his skin hardened from exposure to the elements. But more than that, the strong fingers were quite long, the palms very wide. That hand would cover a lot of territory, and it would hurt — probably worse than any paddle.

She looked up to his face, quickly answering. "No, Sir, I'm not being defiant, and I was never allowed to use such language." She dropped her gaze back to her lap.

"Just what I thought. You know better, bad girl." He sighed. "I won't deal with it right now, but maybe before I bring you back to your bedroll. We'll see."

She hated being called 'bad girl.' What was it about that phrase that made a woman immediately become a chastised five-year-old, losing Daddy's approval? It brought out the guilt and remorse like nothing else said. Yet, her sex throbbed. The promise of being over a man's lap with that large masculine hand so close to her pulsing clit, rubbing and writhing on a denim-covered muscular thigh, reaching for an orgasm made being called 'bad girl' worth it. It'd been a long time since she'd been over a man's lap seeking her release during a spanking.

Startling her back to reality, he sat down next to her on the worn green cot that showed years of hard use. He reached for her hand, clearing his throat. "Now, like I said. I just want to know how you're feeling. I mean...I wanted to see. Are you okay?"

What did he expect her to say? She could be honest with him, tell him she was devastated. Or she could say she was fine. Men seemed to like hearing that women were fine. It meant there was nothing to fix, nothing to do. Carry on.

"I'm fine." She pulled on her skirt, straightening the pleats in it.

"Nope. That's not an answer." He shook his head, scowling at her. "Now, tell me the real answer. How are you?"

Clara sighed loudly. "Are you sure you want the truth? Men say they do, but in the end they really don't."

He nodded. "Yes, I do."

"I'm sad. I'm afraid." She felt the sting of imminent tears. "I don't know what I'm going to do...or even where I'm going to live." The tears tracked down her cheeks, no matter how furiously she swiped at them.

"Ah, hell." He stood up, pulling a handkerchief from his pocket and handing it to her. "I didn't mean to make you cry. But I kinda figured that you'd be having trouble with what happened. I'm having a hard time with what happened." He raked his hands through his dark brown wavy hair in frustration.

"It'd be hard enough to handle this if I was on my own, but to have two little girls relying on me makes this even more difficult." She wiped more tears away. Looking over at Angus, he looked so uncomfortable. He reached out and rubbed her arm a little.

"I know. But nothing changes for now. You'll stay with the Widow Wagon. We'll be going to Oregon Territory and then you can decide if you want to stay there, or come back with me to Missouri again."

"But it wouldn't be decent to ride alone with a man — even if it is the Widow Wagon." She blew her nose, starting to cry aloud. It just seemed so hopeless. She wasn't sure she wanted to live in Oregon, but what choice did she have?

"I'm the wagon master. Women ride to Oregon or back to Missouri with me all the time. I would *never* take advantage of a woman." He stood up and started pacing. "Is that what you're thinking? That I'd hurt you or take advantage of you?" His jaw clenched for a moment.

"No. I know you wouldn't do that. But...what would women say?" She started to wring her hands. "I'm sorry, Angus. It's not you. I just...I don't — what am I going to do?" She threw her hands over her face, sobbing pitifully.

"Oh, hell. I hate a woman cryin'. Shoot." He rubbed her back gently. It had been a long time since she'd been held by a man while she wept. Angus smelled of leather, horses and — man. She nestled her nose into his chest, all the fear, hurt, rejection, and the bitter uncertainty of the future pouring out of her.

She didn't know how long she stayed like that in his

arms, but when the tears and hiccups stopped, she was being lulled and swayed in his arms, feeling soft kisses on the top of her head. She jolted upright, looking around, the amber glow of the candle light making him more handsome than she ever remembered him looking before.

She tugged at her hair, pushing it behind her ear and readjusting her combs. "I'm sorry. I guess I…was more upset than I thought."

Angus cupped her face in his hand. "Clara, don't you dare apologize for feelings. You've had a rough year and what happened today was just…well, it was wrong. That man should be horse whipped. You're a very kind and sensitive woman. Any man would be proud to call you his own."

He stared at her so long that Clara thought he might kiss her. His gaze moved to her lips, staring at them, and then he quickly rose, clearing his throat. "I should get you back to your bedroll. That is, if you feel that you're better. Do you feel better?"

Clara rose. "Yes. I'm fine. Again, I'm sor—"

Angus held up a hand. "I told you not to apologize, and I meant it. Don't push me, girl. I wanted you to share your feelings and you did. There ain't nothin' to feel bad about. I'll take care of you and your girls all the way to Oregon — or to Missouri. Don't you think any more about it. And if any of the women say anything, you let me know. I'll take care of it."

"I will."

"Speaking of which, before you decide to leave. Let's take care of your bad girl language." He sat in her spot on the cot, grabbing her hand before she could leave.

She tried to pull away. "No. I won't do it again. This is just silly."

"Not to me it ain't. It won't be a rough spankin'. Just a reminder. Something to remind you how a lady and a mother is to conduct herself when she speaks." He tugged her over his lap before she had time to escape.

"Angus!" She pushed against his left thigh, trying to squirm her way off his lap. Instead, she felt that hard hand swat her bottom, and even through her skirts, she felt a sting.

"Stop that!" Her skirts brushed against her legs as they were being raised. "I won't bare you, that isn't necessary, but all this damn material will make you think I'm doing nothing. You'll receive these swats on your drawers."

The vast, heavy material had been pushed to the middle of her back and his arm tucked around her waist to pull her into his body. "Very nice, girl. I like the little blue ribbons on the legs and at the waist. You got some pretty fancy drawers."

"Oh, Jesus!" And before she could say anything else he swatted her bottom so hard it took her breath away before she shouted.

"I made the right decision by the looks of it. You're getting a licking for swearing and then swear with your bottom over my knee? What're you thinking?" He swatted the underside of her bottom twice. Hard.

"Ouch! I'm sorry."

"You will be." He then started to swat her bottom, first the left cheek and then the right. The pace and strength of swats increasing until the uncomfortableness of it had her squirming and lifting her feet. She raised her head and started to reach back when he caught her hand, pinning it to her back.

He paused, squeezing her flesh through her pantaloons. "Do you think this reminder will help you keep your mouth under control, girl?"

"Yes, Sir." Her voice broke on the last word. She wasn't crying, but knew she wouldn't be far from it if he didn't stop now.

"Good." He started swatting again, on that sensitive juncture at thigh and bottom. Hard, searing slaps.

She bucked upon his thighs, not caring how lewd it must have looked from his viewpoint. She needed this to end, and she was convinced that waggling her bottom would relieve the pain. Thankfully, at the very moment she feared she'd dissolve into sobs, he stopped. She quickly swiped at the tears that had fallen during the short spanking.

"See? Just a short tanning to your little tail. Now you'll be a good girl for sure." He patted her bottom lightly, pulling her skirts down and helping her to sit on his leg. "You okay?"

Why did men ask that?

No, I'm not okay and you know it. You were the cause of me not being okay!

But like women everywhere, she lied. "Yes, I'm fine."

"I think it's time for this good girl to go to bed. You'll sleep good after your bedtime spankin'." He winked at her, helping her to stand, tucking her into his chest. "Tomorrow will be a new day. It'll be better. You wait and see."

Clara wondered how he stayed so optimistic all the time. Except for getting angry at the antics of the women, he generally was happy and positive.

He opened the flap of the tent, resting his hand on the small of her back as he brought her back to her bedroll. The fire had dwindled down to just embers, and it appeared that all the women had fallen asleep. She had just settled down into her own bag when she sat up. "The girls. I should check on them to make sure they're covered and okay."

He pushed her back down. "You lie down. I'll check on 'em. You do as you're told and go to sleep." He tucked the bedroll around her. "Sleep tight, Clara." He stroked his hand over her hair before walking to the wagon and climbing quietly into it. Rustling could be heard inside, then before she knew it, he'd jumped down, securing the gate again. He mouthed 'okay' to her, before sauntering back to his tent.

She quietly pondered the events of her day, but her last

thoughts were of her warm, freshly spanked bottom, his hard hands and even harder thighs.

It might not be so bad after all being under Angus' care on the journey to Oregon.

CHAPTER THREE

Breakfast had been served, the camp packed up shortly afterward. They'd become pretty adept at packing up the wagon. With the warm, dry air, there was no need to worry about damp bedrolls as they did in the spring rains or heavy dew of Kansas. They'd all been rolled up and put into the wagon, along with the cooking supplies and food stores.

Clara kissed her girls, putting them into the wagon with their dolls with a warning to "behave" when Angus ambled up to them. "Whatcha doin' putting the girls in the wagon? We gotta go sign Independence Rock up there with our names and date." He pointed at the large, rounded rock nearby. It had to be ten times higher than a wagon and Clara guessed you could probably line up forty or more wagons along the length of it. "Besides, the preacher is going to pray over the riders and wagons before we go through South Pass heading West. I'll get the girls for ya."

He snuck up to the wagon, jumping up into it and yelling, making the girls scream and giggle. "C'mon, we're going up to the big rock over yonder and sign our names on it. You'll be part of history." After Angus leapt to the

30

ground, the girls wasted no time jumping out of the wagon into his waiting arms.

Grabbing their hands, he led them back to Clara. "Besides, we need to celebrate, we made it to Independence Rock by Independence Day, just like we needed to. It means we'll be in Oregon, Lord willing, right on time before the cold weather hits."

The pioneers were all crowded around the large, brown rock that rose out of the prairie, using nails and rocks to engrave their names in the granite. It was another gorgeous day in Wyoming, the sky a beautiful blue with only a couple wispy clouds far in the distance. The women would normally be hot walking in the summer sun, but thankfully, a nice breeze blew over the plains to keep them cool.

Just as Angus said, the preacher stood with his large black bible in hand, waiting for the last stragglers — including them — to make their way to the rock so that he could bless the crowd, their wagons, and the livestock. Clara had only met him a few times, but he seemed to be a kind and gentle man with a quiet, caring voice and warm demeanor. Even in the heat, he wore a long black suit coat. Later, she knew he'd have to take that off for the long, hot journey across Wyoming.

Clara couldn't believe she'd made it to Independence Rock. It'd been a long two months and she thought her journey would be ending at this place. Instead, she'd be making her way West with the rest of the crowd gathered at this landmark. This rock marked the end of the prairie voyage and now they'd be crossing mountains and dangerous Shoshone Indian territory for the rest of their journey.

"C'mon in closer, folks. You can sign your name in a minute. First, let me bless y'all before you begin your journey west." He paused, waiting for the men, women, and children to gather quietly around him.

"The Lord has blessed your journey to Independence

Rock. We need to give Him thanks for bringing you to this rock today. There are many who are missing today. Many have died on this journey thus far — from illness, childbirth, injury, drowning, or Indians. You're the blessed people. Let's have a moment of silence to remember those who have passed on to meet the Lord." Everyone solemnly bowed their heads, quietly remembering fellow pioneers.

"Today is the anniversary of the birth of our Nation — Independence Day. It also marks the day all travelers going west are to meet at this rock. You're at the halfway mark. Now, some of you have decided to go back home, and there ain't any shame in knowing what you and your family can handle. If you're going back East today, we ask the Lord to bless you and keep you safe on your journey back."

The crowd murmured their support. Men were seen patting fellow pioneers on the back. Angus shook the hand of a gentleman next to him, wishing him good luck.

Then everyone returned their attention to the preacher. "As a warning before we let you all sign Independence Rock, your journey is typically safe from attack by the Shoshone Indians up to Soda Springs. After that, there have been some pretty gruesome stories of things done to pioneers. Keep close to your wagons and we highly recommend that there be several wagons traveling together. There's safety in numbers. Do *not* get separated from the pack. It may cost you and your family their lives. Make sure you caution your children to stay close to their parents."

Angus jiggled Rose in his arms to get her attention while he tipped Nelly's chin up with his forefinger, whispering, "Did ya hear the preacher? You two need to stay close to the wagon and your ma or me. You don't leave our sight, or go anywhere without holding one of our hands, you hear?" His voice had a stern edge to it that the girls weren't used to hearing from him — at least not directed toward them.

"Yes, Sir," they both mumbled, their large, doe eyes betraying their trepidation at the uncompromising tone in his voice.

"You see that you do. If you don't, there'll be consequences. Do I need to tell you what those consequences might be?"

Nelly, being the oldest, responded for both of them. "No, Sir. We don't like consequences, and I reckon we don't want to talk about them neither."

The corner of his mouth kicked up a little. "See that it stays that way, or we'll be talking for sure." He then turned his gaze to Clara. "And all of the things I just said, they go for you too, girl. Understand?"

"Oh, criminy! I don't need to be scolded like a child, Angus. I know how to stay safe. Why would you even say such a thing to me? Good Lord!" How dare he threaten her in front of her children? She was a grown woman in charge of keeping her own children safe. Why in the world would she wonder off like an aimless fool?

Angus stepped closer, almost nose-to-nose with her. "Because I care about you and your children, and because I want you to remember the switchin' I gave you before." He paused for a second, and she knew she must have looked just as doe-eyed as her own girls had. He could be so firm. "Because, if you wander off alone, even to relieve yourself, you'll be feeling that switch on your bare backside again. Does that answer your question, girl?"

"Yes, Sir." She naturally fell into submitting to him when he took that tone of voice with her. She didn't dare question him, or balk any further.

"And one more thing. Don't take that tone with me. I don't take kindly to it." His eyebrow shot up and her stomach immediately did a flip. She put her hand to her belly, hoping to settle the uneasiness.

"Sorry."

He nodded at her, turning attention back to the

preacher who addressed the crowd.

"...Let us pray. Lord, please bless these people on their travels West. We pray for your protection from pestilence and illness. We ask the Lord to bless all the wagons from mishap, and keep the livestock shoed, watered and fed to bring these good people to their new homes. We ask for protection from death as well. Please send your angels to protect them as they travel from any attacks by Indians. We ask the Lord to bless you and keep you; may He make his face to shine upon you and be gracious to you. May the Lord turn his face toward you and give you peace. Amen."

"Amen," the crowd murmured.

"You all have a blessed journey, and don't forget to sign your names on the Rock before you go!" At that declaration, the children broke free from the ranks and ran to sign their names. Rose struggled in Angus' arms to run after her sister.

"Okay, Rose, hold on a minute before you fall out of my arms." He put her to the ground, laughing when she scrambled away. "Children have a zest for life that we lose as adults. The excitement of writing our names on a rock doesn't thrill us the same way anymore."

"We have other things to worry about. Like where we're going to live or where the next meal is coming from. It's all necessary as you know, Angus." She smiled up at him. Marveling again at how dark his hair and eyes were. He had a scruff on his face from not shaving this morning, and she had to admit it made him more attractive to her. His eyes were so black you couldn't see his pupils, but the laugh lines in his weathered skin gave away the fact that he smiled more than he frowned. He made her feel less lonely — not quite a husband, but more than a friend.

He tucked her under his arm. "I guess you're right, Clara. But let's pretend we're kids for now and scratch our names into this rock too. Whatcha gotta say?"

He made her feel young again. Well, technically, she was still young — but she felt old. Except for today.

Today, she'd laugh and play — even if only for a little while.

"Yes. I'll race ya!" She picked up her skirts and started to run with him yelling behind her.

"No fair! You didn't start the race right. Hell, you didn't even tell me we was gonna race, girl! You better hope I don't catch you." He had a deep, rolling belly laugh and she giggled just hearing it.

Yes, if she couldn't be happy in the long run, she'd be happy playing with Angus — at least for today.

CHAPTER FOUR

Angus had the women gather outside the Widow Wagon, just as the other wagon masters did with their own charges. "You women need to stay close to this wagon. If you need to relieve yourselves or take care of lady business, you need to tell me first that you are leaving — and you *never* go by yourselves. You go in pairs, or a group. But I need to know *first*."

He walked up and down the line of women, keeping his expression serious and his voice stern. He hoped both would frighten each woman into remembering his words and heeding them. If the looks on their faces were any indication — large eyes blinking at him, hands fiddling nervously with skirts — they appeared to be taking him quite seriously indeed.

"You gals don't want to push me on this. I'm serious. This is life and death. I take my responsibility seriously, and I will not tolerate any defiance. I have a nice, sturdy paddle." He reached under the driver's bench seat of the wagon, retrieving a large, wooden paddle. It wasn't long and narrow, but rather round and thick, large enough to address the whole of a woman's bottom quite well. Truthfully, if the sight of the fearsome implement didn't

36

make everyone behave, nothing would. "I haven't had to use it yet. But it'll be waiting for anyone who tries me on this. Questions?" He twirled it in his hand making sure that everyone got to see it up close as he walked by.

He thought the women would just nod mutely, but Minnie cleared her throat and tipped her chin up. Never a good sign.

"So you're saying I can't...do my private business on my own? I have to have one of these people watch me?"

God, women can be so difficult sometimes.

"Well, I never require that they watch you. What I said — which you'd know, if you'd been listening — is that you are to bring another woman with you or go as a group — after you tell me. They can stand at a close distance, but I want you women together so someone can watch for danger. A woman alone out here is in great danger." He walked closer to her. "After you ask permission from me, I'll stand close by so your lookout can yell to me if something isn't right."

"Oh, hell! I'm not going to do that. I'm not doing my necessary with a woman nearby, and I most certainly won't do it with you nearby! I'd rather get taken by Indians, thank you very much." By the time she'd finished her sentence, Angus was standing toe-to-toe with the sassy woman.

"If you don't get taken by Indians or renegades, I'll be painting your bare backside a nice shade of deep red with this paddle." He raised the paddle, holding it up before her, then reached around and swatted her bottom, hard. "You thinking you need some painting done soon, Miss Minnie?"

Minnie grabbed her behind with both hands, then realizing her error, quickly released her bottom, letting her hands hang by her side. She glancing out of the corner of her eyes at the other women, then stared at the dry, dusty ground in front of her. "No, Sir. I just...I don't—"

"Nope. I ain't discussin' this further. Them's the rules.

If you don't follow them, you'll have a meetin' with this paddle. That's it. Nothing to discuss." He slapped the paddle on his hand, the sound cracking through the quiet prairie making the watching women jump. "Let's move out!"

He put the paddle under his seat and hopped up onto his bench, urging the oxen to move forward. It had been a good morning, everyone needed the celebration of making it halfway and commemorating it with their signing of Independence Rock. It meant that they left later than normal, but they'd stop at the trading post at Devil's Gate and spend the night there.

They'd be able to water the oxen, and enjoy the camaraderie of the trading post...before they had to cross rivers, and find more difficult times.

* * *

Minnie had been bitching endlessly about the new rule set forth by Angus. And by the eye-rolling and sighs Clara heard from the other women, they were all a little tired of the complaining.

"Minnie, for crying out loud, you're wearin' us out with your whining! Women do their business in groups anyway. Most of the time we all wander off together to the weeds. What rankles you about this? The fact that he's made it a rule?" Clara knew her exasperation clearly had been evident in her tone, but she didn't care anymore. They'd just gotten rid of Daisy's troublemaking, whining ways, and they didn't need another young lady rising up to take her place.

"I don't like the fact that he thinks one of you silly women would be able to protect me from one of them Indians anyhow."

Clara sighed along with the rest of the women. "Angus said that he'd be close by, so if we see something suspicious, we just signal him and *he* would take care of it. He's the one with the gun. He's just trying to keep us safe."

Minnie stopped walking, tilting her head to the side as if confused. "Wait. Are you and Angus…courting now?"

"What? No! Why would you say that?" Clara's heart began to race. If the women started to attack her over this, it would be a very long trip to the Oregon Territory.

"I think you might be. I saw him taking you to dinner last night. And this morning he stood next to you, holding Rose." Minnie looked to the other women, trying to garner some support for her claims. "If my memory serves me, I think he signed his name near yours too. I think you both may have decided to court — and now we'll be treated like second-class citizens next to you. You'll get favored all the time. Bet he won't paddle or switch *your* ass!"

"You need to take that back! You're just trying to cause trouble, and I ain't havin' it. Daisy tried causing the same trouble with me, and I'm not going to fall into your trap either, Minnie." She stalked off to get away from the women. It would be easier to walk alone than to deal with her trying to rally the others against her.

Caught up in her anger and thoughts, she hadn't noticed that Angus had stopped the wagon and jumped down from the driver's seat. He grabbed her arm, startling her. "What's goin' on here? I can hear yelling, in particular I heard *you* raisin' your voice — which you don't normally do. So what's happening?"

"Nothing. Just women being women. We're fine." She looked up at him to see if he believed her. The narrowing of his eyes told he wasn't buying any of it. "I saw a bee and yelled. That's all."

"Girl, I don't condone lying. I believe that's been discussed on this ride yet. So how about we walk back to the women, and you tell me what's going on?"

"Angus, really it's not necessary. I'm fine. Things are just…fine."

"When women say 'fine,' it's not usually fine at all. Something is going on, enough that you're deciding to not tell me about it — and lie. We're taking care of this right now." He held her by the elbow reluctantly dragging her with him.

When he rounded the back of the wagon, the pale faces turned to him, backs stiffening in alarm.

"Hi, Angus, why are we not moving?" Minnie looked a little too self-satisfied for his liking right about then.

"Since you're the first one brave enough to speak, how about you tell me. Seems like Miss Clara is upset — and she ain't speaking. So I dragged her back here to get some answers."

Minnie's eyes widened infinitesimally for a brief moment. "I'm not sure. We were just talkin', and then she walked away." She turned to look at the other women, batting her eyelashes. "Do any of you recall what we were talking about?"

Angus didn't fall for it; her performance told him that

Minnie had been the instigator. The other women dropped their heads, apparently afraid to say anything more.

"Margie, how about you tell me what happened back here that has Clara so upset." Angus crossed his arms over his chest, his muscles bunching under the worn, thin white shirt, the sleeves rolled up to expose the brawny, deeply tanned forearms.

"I'm not—" Clara started, but he cut her off with a wave of his hand.

"No, I'm talking to *Margie*. You'll have a time to talk too, just not now." He tucked Minnie under his arm, giving her a squeeze before releasing her. Minnie's eyes narrowed, her lips thinning.

Angus thought he had his answer.

Margie quickly glanced at the other women before speaking. "We was walking, listening to Minnie complain about the new rules, and Clara had told her to stop and said that the rules were to protect us. And that's when Minnie decided that you and Clara were courting." Margie looked at both Clara and Minnie, her expression something he couldn't quite place. Was she guilty? Seeking forgiveness? Clara smiled weakly at Margie while Minnie furrowed her eyebrows, scowling her way. How had he missed this personality in Minnie?

Margie took a deep breath before continuing. "Clara told Minnie that you two weren't courtin', but Minnie just kept needling her. Told her that she'd get favored and that you wouldn't switch or paddle Clara if she broke a rule."

Angus stood in front of Minnie with his arms still crossed over his chest, widening his stance, his spurs jangling. "Tell me, Minnie. Who's in charge of the Widow Wagon?"

Her throat worked as she visibly swallowed, confusion shadowing her features. "Uhm...you are, Sir."

"Good. Yes, I am. So, do you get to question what I say or do while on this journey?" He leaned forward. "Mmm?"

"I guess not." She pulled her head back, trying to keep her distance from him.

"You 'guess not'? You're having doubts? Let me help you with that. *No.* The answer is no, you don't get to question what I do." He directed his next remarks to all the women then. "That's not saying you women can't ask me politely. But I'll not condone gossip, backbiting, or stirrin' up trouble when it comes to what I do — or don't do. If you have a problem, you come talk to me directly. Clear?"

The women murmured, nodding in agreement.

"As for anyone breaking rules and not paying the consequences, I don't favor anyone in that regard. Your safety is my responsibility. Period. You put your safety — and my job — at risk, and you'll end up with a fired-up backside." He made sure to stare each woman in the eyes as he said it, letting them know he meant business. Angus would not have a woman killed or injured on his watch. He'd been doing this for three years and hadn't had one incident yet and he intended to keep it that way too.

Minnie spoke up.

Again.

"So are you saying…that you and Clara ain't courtin'?"

It looked like she was still angling to cause trouble…which would more than likely end with her backside being introduced to his paddle.

He stepped close to her again, towering over her by at least a foot. "Missy, you and I are gonna tangle at this rate. I ain't answering to you or anyone else about anything unrelated to the wagon, 'cuz it ain't none of your business. End of discussion, girl!"

Angus turned on his heel, walking away. He stopped suddenly in his tracks, striding back toward them. "And one more thing. I want all the gossiping to stop. *Now.* And if you don't follow the rules — any of ya — you'll pay the price."

He marched away, grabbing Clara's hand and leading

her to the front of the wagon. He hated people picking on others, and he meant what he said — he wouldn't tolerate it. But he knew that what made him fume more than anything was that it involved Clara — and by association — her girls. It had been a while since he'd felt that protective of someone. He knew the feelings were mutual. He just wasn't quite sure how he'd proceed with this. Until he did decide though, those damn spiteful women weren't going to wound her any further.

"Angus, I shouldn't be up here with you. She'll start talking again." Clara craned her head around to look back toward the rear of the wagon.

"Don't you dare kowtow to that wildcat." He grabbed her chin, forcing her to meet his gaze. "I need you to keep me informed if this continues. I meant what I said — I'm not tolerating it. You — or the girls — could be hurt by this."

"Yes, Sir. But all of...this." She waved her hand through the air. "This has probably made it worse."

He tilted his head at her. Was she angry at him? "'This is me taking care of you, protecting you and the girls both. Women, as you know, can be spiteful. I had to put my foot down to nip this in the bud."

"I know." She dropped her gaze, playing with the ribbon from her bonnet. "It's just...they'll see this as favoring me again."

The concern in her eyes tugged at his heartstrings. He hated seeing the worry etched on her face. "Would that be a bad thing? Me favorin' you and the girls?"

She blinked, staring at him, obviously trying to read his intentions. He hoped she'd see it for what it was — him liking her and wanting to go further. "Do you?"

He nodded, feeling a blush rise on his own face, like he was a damn teenager. Jesus, why did stuff like this have to happen around women, especially one he liked?

"Yeah, I do favor you and the girls. I'd like to see where this takes us. How's that sound to you?" His heart galloped in his chest. Would his boss, Charlie, at the Widow Wagon, view this as inappropriate? He hoped not.

The hell with it. I'll deal with that when I get back to Missouri. If I get back to Missouri.

"I like you, and the girls do too. I think we could be happy, but——"

"Nope. Not buts. We need to do what we want without regard to anyone else." He pulled her into his embrace. "I think we're officially courtin', Miss Clara. Now, they can talk and it'll be the truth."

Clara looked to see if any of the women were watching, pushing on his chest to give herself distance. "Shhh! God, my life may actually become hell."

He tipped her chin up. "In more ways than one if you don't tell me if they give you trouble. You'll be sittin' on a tender hind-end for a while. Keep it in mind."

"Yes, Sir."

Angus kissed her forehead. "We best get going. I'll see you later tonight at the campfire." He winked her way before jumping up to sit on the wagon driver's bench. It had been a long time since his heart skipped a beat like it had just now, and he felt like cheering. It felt good to be happy, his cock jerking to life, confirming that other parts of him were in full agreement.

CHAPTER FIVE

As promised, when they left Independence Rock, the first day was a shorter journey. They made it to Devil's Gate well before nightfall. The two stones were so impressive jutting out the ground—a gorge for the Sweetwater River. Clara had heard one of the wagon masters say that the rocks were five hundred feet high. The rumbling roar of Sweetwater River racing through the crevice and smashing against the sandstone at the bottom was deafening. The divide was so shallow that only one wagon would be able to go through at a time but it widened at the top. Thankfully, it wasn't an issue; they'd be going around Devil's Gate, not through it. But they'd follow the river.

The trading post was in the center of town, and there were buildings everywhere selling their wares. There were furriers selling pelts from various animal, farriers selling horseshoes, blacksmiths selling wheels, nails, and other parts for wagons for the journey West. Other buildings sold blankets, coats, mittens, hats, and underthings for men and women to keep them warm. For many of the pioneers it would be their last chance to stock up on oxen shoes, nails, and other supplies before the next leg of the route out to Soda Springs.

The wagons made camp around the outskirts of the trading post, keeping close even though the threat of Indian attack was almost nonexistent in that part of Wyoming. The Shoshone were known to be peaceful. It was after Soda Springs that you had to worry.

Sam, the cook for the Widow Wagon and second in command under Angus, yelled to the children. "I want all the young'uns and women to start looking for buffalo chips. We ain't havin' dinner until I can start a fire. So you better get along!"

Due to the lack of trees, they used buffalo dung to cook their dinners. The women and children gathered them while walking during the day and then again when they set up their camp sites.

Clara gathered the girls and started to walk toward the Widow Wagon women, intending to join the search. Immediately, Minnie rolled her eyes and lifted her chin, turning away. Clara steeled herself, taking a deep breath. She'd not let Minnie get to her. This had been a good day. Her spirit felt light and easy for the first time in weeks, and cattiness would not ruin it.

She walked up to the women. "Hope we can find enough. It gets pretty picked over at some stops."

Margie picked her head up from searching. "You got that right. I've only picked up four. Hope we don't have to walk too far."

Lizzie smiled sweetly at her. She enjoyed Lizzie. Although thirty, she seemed much younger. She and her husband had never had children — or at least she assumed so. Clara felt a little sad thinking about that, knowing Lizzie would have made a wonderful mother. She played with Nelly and Rose, and did a little stitching with them around the campfire at night. She only had a little cloth and a needle and thread that she picked up at one of their stops, but in the evening, her girls loved learning the new stitches with her.

"I thought you'd be back at the wagon relaxing with Angus," Minnie said, practically spitting the venomous words. "Didn't think he'd make you pick up buffalo shit with the rest of us."

"Angus wouldn't treat me different. I'll get in trouble and get my ass spanked just like the rest of you."

"So are you two courtin' or not? He wouldn't say. Just kept saying it was none of my business." At that point, the other women all turned their stares her way and Clara felt compelled — though she knew it probably wasn't the smartest idea — to answer, and answer honestly.

"We weren't before. But we are now." She bent over to pick up a buffalo chip at her feet, depositing it in her apron.

"I knew it! Now the rest of us will be just *servants* to you two. It ain't right. I'm thinking that the Widow Wagon wouldn't want him gallivanting with any loose trollop on the wagon either."

Clara didn't remember exactly what happened, but Minnie's spiteful words had been like waving a red flag in front of a bull. All she remembered was sitting on top of Minnie's back, pulling on her hair with all her might. Once her hands were full of her dark hair and Minnie's strident shouts could be heard over most of Wyoming, she stood again, fishing the webbed hair out from between her fingers, letting the torn locks float in the warm afternoon breeze on the dusty plain.

Minnie stood up, her face red and dusty from wailing while face down in the dirt. "You're despicable! I refuse to talk to you or be anywhere near you from now on." She spun on her heel, directing the next phrase to the other women. "I'm going back to the post. You women can gather your chips without me." She stalked away, leaving a dust trail behind her as her skirts brushed through the dry sand.

Clara looked over at the other women as they all watched Minnie storm off toward the wagons.

"Don't pay her no mind. She's just acting immature. She nothing but a child, and a spoiled one at that." Margie walked up to her, putting her arm around Clara and pulling her in for a hug. "I'm glad that Angus has taken a shine to ya. You two make a good pair, I'm thinking. And he adores your little girls. They'll enjoy having a pa again, I'm sure."

"Well, we ain't talkin' marriage or nothin', but yes, they'll be happy if it becomes more." She swiped at the tears on her face, the grit from the dusty air smearing across her cheeks.

"I think it's right nice. I mean the way you was left at the station, and all. It shows that Angus must have felt sad that you was leavin'. Don't ya think?" Lizzie rubbed her arm, looking unsure as to whether she should hug her or not.

Clara pulled her into her embrace. "You're both being so sweet. I think you might be right, Lizzie." She gathered up the buffalo chips that scattered from her apron when she charged at Minnie. "It feels nice to be happy. I get that fluttery feeling when he walks by or winks at me, ya know?"

They giggled. "I reckon I can recall that feelin'. Been a coon's age since I felt it, but I've been in love before too." Margie sniggered, elbowing Clara.

It felt good to laugh with the women, especially after the ruckus with Minnie. Angus would be livid if he heard about it. She wondered if she should say something, or just keep quiet hoping he wouldn't find out. She had a funny feeling that Angus wouldn't cotton to her neglecting to tell him, and she was fairly certain he'd see it as a form of lying. She'd tell him as soon as she got to camp. Besides, he'd told her to let him know if Minnie gave her any more trouble.

"I don't imagine Angus is going to be too happy when he finds out that I pulled half of Minnie's hair out."

"You aren't going to tell him, are ya?"

The surprise in Lizzie's voice made Clara actually contemplate keeping it hidden — until Margie spoke up. "Of course, she isn't going to hide it. Angus needs to know what she called you. He might not like that you pulled her hair, but I'm betting he'll be madder at Minnie for calling you a trollop and insinuating that Angus would sleep with a trollop."

It was at that point that Angus galloped up to them on his horse. "Someone spotted Shoshone in the distance. Git back to camp." He looked around. "Where's Minnie?"

The womens' gazes skittered Clara's way then back to the ground. Clara took a deep breath. "Well, her and I had a tussle of sorts — and she stormed off saying she was going back to the trading post."

"Tussle?" He pushed his tattered, dirty work hat back on his forehead. "What kinda tussle are we talking about?"

He had that uncompromising tone to his voice.

"She called me a trollop and said that the Widow Wagon might want to know that you gallivant with trollops."

His eyes narrowed and that tic in his jaw came out as it did when he was pushed to his limit. Clara quickly continued before he leapt off the horse to tan her hide. "I kinda had a conniption of sorts, and I tackled her to the ground, pulling out handfuls of hair. But...I stopped. I stopped myself Angus, I swear. I didn't do anything else."

He chuckled, crossing his hands over the saddle horn. "Guess I always knew you could take care of yourself after seein' what you did to Daisy. Seems to me that Minnie deserved more, and you stopped yourself from fighting or switching her like you did Daisy. I'd say you learned your lesson. Good Girl."

"You're...not mad?" Clara didn't want to push it, but she couldn't quite believe what she'd just heard. Relief flooded through her when she realized he wouldn't be paddling her after all. Still, she was shocked that he seemed to approve of her actions.

"I still don't like you fighting. But what she said was uncalled for. I can't talk about this any longer. We'll discuss this later." He narrowed his eyes at the women as he spoke. "I need to find that spoiled brat before the Indians find her. You all run back to camp. Now!"

He rode off toward the trading post to find Minnie, and Clara felt a twinge of guilt. If the woman — spiteful or not — got hurt because of this, she would never forgive herself.

The three women held their skirts off the ground, wrapping their aprons around the gathered buffalo chips, and ran to the safety of the wagons and the other pioneers.

Sam stood waiting for them, corralling them into the wagon with the children. "Where in tarnation is Minnie?"

Clara threw her arms around the girls. "Angus went to find her. She stormed off toward the wagons. Other than that we don't know where she is."

"Jesus. It ain't even been twenty-four hours since we told you not to leave alone." He shook his head, closing the gate to the wagon. "Someone's gettin' paddled today, for sure." All the women exchanged looks. Clara felt bad for Minnie — and felt a bit responsible for her going missing too.

"Mama, you're not getting paddled, are you?" Nelly chewed on her bottom lip.

"No, sweetie. Mama's fine."

Rose spoke up. "Sounds like Mister Angus is using that really big paddle on Miss Minnie, Nelly."

"Shhh! Both of you. It isn't none of your business. Mind what you're doing — or not doing."

Silence descended over the wagon then. Between the threat of attack from the natives and the threat of an angry Angus, the women were lost in their own thoughts. Clara knew she should be more frightened of the Indian attack, but her concern about Angus and the threat of that paddle smacking against delicate flesh crowded away all other thoughts.

Angus truly was like a bear — large, formidable, growly, and just by walking into a room made his presence known. But when push came to shove, he loved rolling in the grass, playing and enjoying the comforts of friends, family and the great outdoors.

Poking that large bear definitely had been a grave error on Minnie's part. She'd be on the receiving end of that growly bear's anger before the night was over.

* * *

D*amn women!*
Days like this made him question his sanity. Who else would travel three thousand miles with eight women in a fucking covered wagon across prairies, plains, deserts, floods, raging rivers --- all with the ever-present threat of Indian attack.

He leapt off his horse, walking behind the row of wooden buildings at the trading post. "Minnie Johnson, you better get your skinny tail out here! Now!" He stomped past the buildings, looking down the alleyways as he passed each one. Seeing something move, he backed up and walked down one of them, between the Saloon and the Blacksmith's building.

Found you!

He snatched her up from behind some crates on the side of the building. "Didn't you hear me callin' ya?" He shook her lightly.

"Yes. But I was afraid."

"You have every right to be afraid. But not answering, just added five more swats of my paddle."

Her eyes widened, her face going pale, throat working. "I...are you...I'm getting *paddled?*"

"Hell yes! I just told you women to stay close to each other not more than eight hours ago — and you just walked off. The Shoshone were spotted in the distance, and I couldn't find you because you disobeyed." He began walking back the way he'd come, dragging her along behind him. "You won't do it again, neither. Trust me."

"But—" Minnie started to whine.

"Nope. Not hearin' it. There's no need for discussion. There isn't anything you can say that'll stay my hand." He didn't even look at her as he said it. She'd receive no comfort from him until he tanned her ass good. She had put everyone at risk, him included. It wasn't fair to the others. A lesson needed to taught — and he would be the one teaching it.

When they were close enough to the wagon for other

pioneers to hear and see his next actions, he swatted her backside a couple times, sending her bounding toward the wagon. "Now get in that wagon and think about the paddling coming to you when I get back." She ran to the wagon, clambering up and over the gate to join the other women.

The men stationed themselves around their wagons, guns drawn, scanning the horizon for any movement or sign of Shoshone. It always amazed Angus how noisy a circle of wagons could be. Between the children playing, women talking and laughing, cooking utensils clattering, it could be very chaotic and loud. But in situations like this, the quiet was almost deafening. Not one sound, not even from the oxen and horses. The occasional hawk or eagle would soar above, but everything stood still except the constant breeze.

After they stood like that for a while, waiting, a couple scouts were sent out to check the distance again. They finally whistled an all clear and people scrambled out of their wagons, picking right up with what they were doing before the scare.

That is except for the Widow Wagon.

The women there were apparently scared enough — either of him or the Shoshone — that they sat huddled together like naughty children awaiting their fate. He pulled the gate down on the back of the wagon, the chains rattling.

He slapped his hand on the thick gate, startling the women. "Minnie! Front and center! And Clara, you come too."

CHAPTER SIX

He watched the women hop out, directing them to stand to his right. Then he yelled to the rest. "I want the rest of you out here too."

The women came out one-by-one, each looking as unsure as the woman before her. They filed into a line, side-by-side without further direction. Nelly and Rose came to the edge of the wagon last. Rose had tears tracking down her cheeks, quietly crying. She was such a sweet little pumpkin. While Nelly had her lip between her teeth — just like her mother did when she felt concerned or wary.

"Well, c'mon," he said, reaching up to help them down. Nelly just stared at him, not moving. Rose shook her head, her lip trembling. "I don't want to. Are we getting paddled?"

"What?"

Oh, Lord.

Angus felt awful. Why would they even think that? He'd never said anything about punishing them when he put them in the wagon. "What makes you think you'd be paddled, sweetheart?"

"You're so angry, and you're not 'Mister Angus.'" Rose

closed her eyes then, and sobs started to wrack her little chest.

"Oh, darlin'. I'm always Mister Angus." His voice softened and he motioned for her to come forward. She ran toward him, jumping into his arms. "You are *not* getting paddled. One of the women over here will be getting her tail tanned today. Now, you dry those little tears, and Mister Sam will bring you over to the Anderson wagon so you can play with the other kids." He used the pads of his thumbs to wipe the tear tracks from her pudgy cheeks.

He'd been told many times that he was too soft when it came to women or children crying. He couldn't help it. It just tore him up. The urge to fix whatever was wrong and put a smile back on their faces tugged at him so hard it felt like he couldn't breathe right until things has been put to rights. The need to comfort, console and protect those weaker than himself proved much stronger than his need to keep order and discipline. Although he refused to tolerate defiance either, he struggled internally with meting out the consequences when they were needed.

He put Rose on the ground and motioned for Nelly to jump into his arms. She smiled, jumping at him. "You've both been such good girls. You listen and do as you're told — every day." He kissed Nelly's cheek, squeezing her into a bear hug, putting her down next to her sister. "No more tears. You both find your friends and run and play." As they ran off, he shouted, "You listen to Mr. Anderson and do as you're told."

Nelly shouted back. "We will, Mister Angus." And they were giggling and carefree once again. If only adult problems could be handled so easily. He watched until Tiny Anderson turned and waved to him.

Now to deal with the…big girls. Minnie had been a quiet passenger until Daisy exited the wagon at Chimney Rock. He wondered how Daisy was doing with her new husband, Noah. That woman had been enough trouble for three men. However, that Scandinavian mountain of a man had appeared more than capable to handling her. Daisy's personality must have overshadowed the other women enough on the journey that Angus hadn't noticed the troublesome Minnie had a little bit too much spunk in her. He had no doubt Noah would've had to assert his authority immediately with Daisy, make it clear in her mind who was really in charge. Usually a few good, hard swats of the paddle made that clear.

Angus walked past the women up to the front bench, reaching under it to grab his maple paddle. He'd been told on more than one occasion from his wife that she hated that paddle more than anything else he'd used on her — well, everything but the buggy whip. He twirled it in his hand as he passed them again.

"Minnie and Clara, over here."

They both stared at him with huge round eyes.

"Now!"

They rushed forward until they stood in front of him. "Did I or did I not tell you women — just this morning — to not go *anywhere* alone?"

"Yes, Sir," they mumbled in unison.

"Mmm, I thought so too." He rubbed his palm over the smooth wood. "Minnie, I hear tell that you said I like — what was that phrase?" He made a show of stroking his chin, and looking up to the sky, as if he couldn't recall the words — then snapping his fingers as if he'd suddenly remembered. "Oh yes, 'gallivanting with trollops.' Is that what you said?"

She glared at Clara, then looked back at him. "I did. But you're missing the rest."

"First, don't you glare at her again. Clear?" He wagged his finger at her. He'd have none of this, especially now that Clara was his — or would be his soon.

"Yes."

"Nope. Try again." She needed a lesson in respect, right quick.

"Yes, *Sir*." He nodded. "I heard the rest already. You said that Clara was a trollop and that Charles might want to know that I was galavantin' with trollops. I don't think there's anything else I need to hear."

"Clara ain't innocent, neither." She rubbed her hands through her hair, pulling out clumps of torn locks to show him. "She pulled handfuls of my hair out. I still have a headache."

"That headache won't be bothering you for long. You'll be receiving another kinda pain to keep you distracted from that."

He walked up to Clara. It was time to teach his girl a little lesson too. "So you pulled her hair out?"

She lifted her gaze from the dry brown dirt at her feet to look him straight in the eye.

Good girl.

"Yes, Sir, I did."

He liked a woman with spunk, and honesty was an important quality to him. Clara had both. She hadn't lied when she fought with Daisy either. "You were punished for switching Daisy. Do you think you should be paddled for pulling Minnie's hair out — as she said — 'in clumps?'"

Her gaze flitted toward Minnie, who was still rubbing her scalp and pouting dramatically. "I don't make those decisions, Sir. It would be up to you to decide."

And that was his good girl, submitting to his authority. "Did you think about getting paddled if you fought with Minnie — and then decided to do it anyway?"

This would be the telling answer. If she said yes, then he'd have no choice but to paddle her for defiance — knowing the rule and consequences, but doing it anyway.

"No, Sir. I just...I guess I just reacted to being called a trollop." She pulled that worried lip between her teeth.

Poor girl.

He leaned forward until they were nose-to-nose. "As you should have. You don't let anyone call you a trollop."

He chucked her under the chin, winking before he walked away. "Good girl."

"Now, Miss Minnie." He stood in front of her now. "You appear to have quite a list of infractions, it seems. Name-calling, instigating a fight, and the worst of them all, separating yourself from the women. Oh, and not coming when you were called. That's quite a list, don't ya think?"

"I guess."

"I guess so too. When you ran off, did you think about the rule I'd given just this morning?" He'd be anxious to see what her answer was. It would be telling.

"I reckon...I don't want to say."

He narrowed his eyes. "Guess that's my answer then. I'll take that as a yes. *Bad girl.*" He placed his paddle on the gate, picking Minnie up by the waist, resting her on her belly so her hips were at the edge. "Pull your skirts up so only your drawers are exposed."

A low whine came from her, but her hands came back, slowly dragging up the several layers of cloth, her fingers struggling to get all the layers gathered into her small hands.

Once they were pulled up, he pushed the material further up her back, resting the paddle on her bottom. Her pristine white flesh shown through thin cotton pantaloons embellished with little pink bows and ribbons. He swore the material looked wet near her quim. She wouldn't be the first woman to drench her pussy in anticipation of a punishment.

"Now, we'll talk." He slapped her bottom, and she groaned in response. "There have been terrible stories of people lost, or killed on these trails. I hear tell that recently a woman disappeared — and it turned out she'd been snatched by the Shoshone. She's still there as a squaw to the Chief of that tribe. Is that what you were wanting, Miss Minnie?"

"No, Sir." He swatted each thigh twice, hard, and she cried out at each slap.

"She's the lucky one. Many are just killed and left for the buzzards or wolves, their scalps hanging on poles. You thought it hurt to get clumps taken out? Imagine having your scalp cut off." He gave her several hard swats to the crest of her bottom — first left, then right, then the center.

"Oh no! I'm sorry!" She reached back, trying to cover her bottom.

"And there are stories of women captured by renegades who steal women from the trail so they can obtain money for their return. Most of these women are raped and beaten while they're with these criminals." He landed four more crisps slaps to her thighs. "Am I gettin' through to you, Minnie?"

"Yes, Sir. Stop!"

"I'm just getting started. This is just your warm-up, girl." He walked away, leaving her to soothe her flesh. "As I said this morning, your safety is my responsibility, and regardless of what you said, I do *not* gallivant with women — and I definitely don't traipse around with trollops. You *will* mind my rules. I won't have you gettin' yourself killed or kidnapped on my watch."

"But, I—"

"Nuh uh. I think it's time for my paddle to do the rest of the talking." He picked up the gleaming, polished wood, slapping it against his hand to set the tone. It was always good for a woman to feel a little trepidation and fear right at the beginning. It made things worthy of remembering, after the fact. He grasped the ruffled elastic waistband, tugging her pantaloons down to her shoes, leaving her exposed and bare to both the warm breeze and the gazes of the gathered pioneers.

She put her hands over her face, quietly crying before it even started. "Your bottom is nice and pink already. You mark easily. Something for me to remember." He patted her haunches. "Have you ever been paddled, girl?"

"Yes, Sir." She sniffled pathetically, and he felt himself hesitating a little. He needed to start this though, so he didn't back down. This was necessary for her to learn a lesson — so they'd all be safer. Disciplining her in front of the women would be important for them too, something that would reinforce his words of warning.

"Since you've been paddled before, then you know what to expect. No hands, no biting, no swearing." He tucked an arm around her waist, further ensuring that she wouldn't reach back and injure her hands or a finger. He started with solid, slow swats, letting the heat and sting sink in before the next slap. He steadily punished her bottom until it no longer looked pink, but red. She began to cry and squirm her hips, trying to avoid the bite of the maple.

"Do you think the paddle is giving you a good lesson?" He stroked a hand over her flesh, which felt warm to the touch. She'd be feeling this tomorrow — if not longer.

"Y-Yes, Sir." He rubbed her back, letting her catch her breath before giving her the final flurry of harder swats to reinforce the lesson and make it memorable.

"Tell everyone here looking at your naughty bottom why you're getting blistered today."

She keened low and long, taking in a deep breath. "I spoke ill of Angus and C-Clara. I wandered off-f-f on my own, put my safety at r-risk, and caused a f-fight."

"Quite a list you got there, naughty girl. It's a whole lot easier takin' the cat out of the bag than puttin' it back, huh?" He rubbed the scalded flesh, moving her hands out of the way when she tried to reach back.

"Yes, Sir."

"I thought you'd see it my way. Let's finish this spanking so you can be in right standing again." He tucked her body to him tightly, knowing the struggle would be more intense. She screeched before he even started spanking.

He took a deep breath, gathering his resolve. Remembering that she could've been kidnapped reignited his frustration, his determination. Her bottom was a deep red and he knew she already had to be on a simmer with pain — which he'd be setting to a boil soon. He gripped the blonde paddle and peppered her bottom with a flurry of swats, that hard, unforgiving wood leaving her writhing and a screaming.

"The next time I give an order, you're going to listen and obey! What you want to do does not matter out here. You *will* do as you're told. Clear?"

Her feet were kicking up, her pussy peeking through the tuft of curly chestnut brown hair at the juncture of her thighs, as well as her pink, little back hole.

"Yes! I will!" she yelled loudly.

"See that you do!" He gave her a dozen more rapid swats, given so fast and hard that she had no time between them to do anything but wag her head back and forth as she cried.

While she sobbed in obvious despair, he continued. "And these last five are for not coming when you were called."

He laid down those five strokes just as hard and fast, though this time all of them were to her thighs. Her feet fluttered frantically as if she meant to swim away from him. When he stopped, she lay sobbing forlornly upon the gate. Her face rested upon weathered, gray wood wet with a puddle of her own tears.

He walked past the women, paddle in hand, returning it to its rightful place up front. Once he returned to her side, he patted her bottom before yanking the pantaloons back up over her well-spanked bottom, pulling the skirts back down, and helping her off the gate. He kept his hands around her waist until her wobbly legs found their strength again.

"You okay?" He tilted his head to look her in the eye.

"Yes, Sir. I'll be good. I promise." He pulled her to his chest. "I'm sure you will, Minnie."

He looked at the other women, barking at them. "You all go finish your chores. Minnie is excused from any further work tonight."

The women quickly left, no doubt anxious to be anywhere else at that moment.

"Let's get you up into the wagon so you can go to sleep." He placed his hands at her waist to hoist her up.

"Angus, wait. I need to...I have to relieve myself."

"C'mon then. Let's get you over behind those rocks first."

She stopped dead in her tracks. "I can't do *that* with you near."

"You have no choice, girl. I ain't lettin' you go alone." He raised his eyebrows at her, putting his hands on his hips. "Are you asking for another spanking? Is that what you want?"

"No! I just..." She literally was wringing her hands. Women amazed him. She'd just been paddled a dark shade of red, and Indians were everywhere, but she worried about a man being ten feet away while she emptied her bladder.

"C'mon, girl. You'll be fine." He took the choice away from her, and like most women when faced with no options, she complied easily.

He brought her to the area the pioneers used to relieve themselves near the stream behind some rocks for privacy not far from the wagons. Angus stood on the other side of the rocks waiting for her. Before long her quiet cries could be heard. "You all right, Minnie?"

"It hurts to bend over."

He winced at the twinge of guilt, but he wouldn't let her know that. "As it should if I did my job right. It'll be a good reminder for you to behave." He'd have to check on her tonight to see how she was. Might have to rub some liniment on it.

Damn.

But he couldn't have her putting them all at risk.

She rounded the stones, walking up to him, her face still red from all the crying — or perhaps embarrassment.

Angus wrapped his arm around her shoulders. And even though it was still evening, and they hadn't had dinner yet, Angus knew she'd fall asleep after her paddling. "You'll feel better after you rest for a couple hours. I'll save you a plate of dinner."

Angus climbed into the wagon first, moving burlap and canvas bundles aside, throwing a blanket on the hard bed of the wagon, making a bed for Minnie to sleep on. Once it looked comfortable and he'd found a pillow inside a trunk, he hopped down and helped Minnie climb up into the wagon. He covered her with a light blanket.

"I hate that I had to punish you like that. I don't like making any of you women cry. Please make sure you behave so it don't have to happen again. Ya hear?"

"I will. I promise." Her heavily-lidded eyes had already started to blink slowly. She'd be asleep in no time.

He jumped from the wagon and went behind the saloon and blacksmith buildings, just to the left of the wagon area to have a smoke. The women didn't realize how much it bothered him to have these sessions. However, on his way to the same alley he had found Minnie in, he changed his mind and slipped into the saloon instead for a shot of whiskey, and a smoke.

He'd make it back in time for dinner.

CHAPTER SEVEN

C lara felt bad for Minnie, just as she had with Daisy. She knew how stern and harsh Angus could be when provoked. And as bad as she felt for her, she couldn't help but feel relieved that he'd let her off with just a scare. Later in the evening, after it had been dark for a couple hours, Clara tucked her girls in for the night, sleeping near Minnie. She told them to not whisper or giggle. They were to go straight to sleep so Minnie wouldn't wake up.

"Mama, I don't want Mister Angus to ever be that angry at me." Nelly's eyes were huge. Rose had her thumb in her mouth which she did when something upset her, even though she'd been supposedly broken of the habit prior to her father's death.

"If you do as you're told, Mister Angus won't have any reason to be upset with you. Besides, you girls are children — Angus seems pretty patient with children. Don't you worry about it none. It's time to sleep. Do *not* wake up Minnie."

She set up the bedrolls around the fire and tidying the campsite. Then she felt a touch to her arm, Angus' deep, male voice seeming to rumble in her chest.

"Miss Clara, come with me, please."

She quickly looked to see if any of the women had noticed. Fortunately, none seemed to have stirred.

"Don't you worry about them," Angus said. "I think after today, the women won't question you again."

"Well, I don't want them thinking I'm getting treated differently." She tucked a stray lock of hair behind her ear.

"I should hope I treat you different. I'm not courtin' the other women." He opened the flap of his tent, letting her in before him. He waved her toward the cot.

She sat staring at him, while he poured some water into battered tin cups. "I don't have anything other than whiskey and water. I'm assuming that you don't want any whiskey." He stopped mid-pour, waiting for her answer.

"No. Water is fine, Angus." She took a sip, resting her cup on the ground near her feet. "Is there a reason I'm here?"

"I think it's time we just sit and talk, find out more about each other. Hold hands, and such. The way couples do when they court." He looked uncomfortable, as if he wasn't sure what to do with his hands or feet. He seemed to dwarf the tent. She knew he was large, but in the great expanse of the outdoors he didn't seem as imposing as he did in the confines of his quarters.

"Let's start with talking about our families, our spouses. How they died. Things like that." He pulled his chair closer to her. "You share first."

Clara shared how Matthew had died from dropsy. How they had known he'd been declining in his health. It'd been a rough year for them all. She related how each of the girls had dealt with his death and their excitement at starting anew with a new home and father.

They continued talking well into the night, after the normal evening din of a bustling pioneer camp had long since given way to the silence of the night.

It then became Angus's turn to relate how his wife and girls had died. He told her how he had cared for them, relating his heartbreak and sitting in that cold cabin for four days after they had died, with no memory of the time lapse. He shared each of the girl's personalities. The tears flowed when he relayed how sweet and cuddly his Prissy was and how she was Daddy's girl. And they laughed when he relayed some of the antics of Kat.

She swiped at the tears on her face, her heart breaking for Angus and his loss. Suddenly, Clara became aware how quiet the campsite had become.

"My Lord, Angus. How late is it?" She looked at his wrist to see if he had his watch on him.

He pulled his pocket watch out. "It's ten thirty."

Clara jumped up, putting a hand to her neck.

Dear Lord, it's guaranteed the women will gossip now.

"Oh, Angus. This isn't good. I've been in here too long."

"Clara, sit." When she continued to stand staring at him, he barked louder. "Now."

"Don't yell at me, Angus." How dare he yell at her when she was only concerned about their reputation?

"Who do you think you're talking to, girl?" He stood now too, lowering his voice and whispering, which seemed much more frightening than his raised voice. "Sit, Clara. While you still can."

Her bottom quickly met the cot, she looked up at his hulking form standing over her. "Care to explain why you're so panicked?"

"No. I'm fine." She brushed at her skirt. He'd dismiss what she had to say anyway.

"Stand up." She stood hesitantly, gasping when he jerked her by her elbow and landed two crisp swats to her bottom. "Talk to me."

She fought the urge to rub her bottom. How his hand could still hurt this much even through her skirts, she would never understand. "The women…will talk. They'll be whispering while we're bathing or walking tomorrow. Or even worse, they'll be quiet and not speaking at all —

as women do."

"So. Ignore them. What we do is none of their business."

She rolled her eyes so hard it hurt.

"Girl, don't roll your eyes at me unless you want more of those swats I just gave you." She didn't, so she nodded at him quietly. "I like you, Clara, and I like the girls. I'd like to see where this will go, but I think we'll be moving quickly. It kinda feels like maybe this is more than just luck, like there's been a divine intervention of sorts. Does that make sense to you? Or is it just me?"

Clara had been thinking this for the past couple days, but had been afraid to feel it let alone form it into words. "I've thought the same thing. Do you think it's too soon?"

"How? Yesterday you were going to marry a man you'd never met. I've known you for almost two months now."

That was the cold, honest truth. She had been prepared to marry a stranger, yet she found herself hesitating with Angus. After listening to his story and how his family died, she had no doubt in her mind as to the type of father and husband he would be to her and the girls.

"I guess, you're right. I didn't know Eugene at all. The girls have grown so fond of you — and I have too."

He enveloped her small hand in his; it felt like the whole of her hand fit into his huge palm. "How about we look for a preacher in the morning and get hitched? Will you marry me, Clara?" He dropped to his knee, kissing the top of her hand. "I know it feels quick, but I believe this union will be blessed. I promise to be the best husband and father I can be."

"Yes! Yes, Angus. I'll marry you!" She threw her arms around his neck as he rose in front of her. He picked her up, spinning her in circles.

"I can't remember the last time I felt this happy." He kissed her forehead, tilting her chin, pressing her lips to his, the touch soft and feathery. Then with a fevered inhale, he plundered her mouth, kissing her roughly, drawing her closer to his body. She moaned and his tongue slipped into her mouth, poking and rubbing the inside of her. The material of her corset felt rough against her suddenly hard nipples. His hands cupped her bottom, and he pulled her close, growling in her mouth, his hands raking through her long hair, tightly gripping it in his fists, the tugs on her scalp igniting her passion.

He pulled away, sighing in frustration. He traced gentle, slow kisses down her neck, her collar bone, working his way back up to her mouth. She looked at his face — he was so handsome, the dark hair and his dark eyes now hooded with arousal. It was then that she realized the intensity of his stare, almost too intense.

"What? Why are you looking at me that way? I know...I'm not young and beautiful anymore. I've been through a lot, so I look worn and—"

He pulled her to his chest and swatted her bottom several times. "If you speak like that again, I'll spank your backside. Do you hear me? You're beautiful and I'll make sure you know it every day." Then he covered her mouth with his, his lips soft and sensual. This time he kissed slowly and softly, her belly flipping, her sex throbbing with need. He jerked away from her. "We need to stop. I can't keep going like this."

His hand raked through his hair. "I gotta get you to bed. We'll be up early tomorrow, telling everyone about the wedding and you becoming Missus Angus." He waggled his eyebrows at her. "Has a nice ring to it, don't it?"

"What is your last name, Angus?"

"Warren. Angus Warren."

"Clara Warren," she whispered. "I like the sound of it."

He chuckled. "Good, cuz I can't see myself having a different name." He pecked her on the lip, then her forehead, his hands cupping her head gently. "Let's get you to bed."

As suspected, the women were sound asleep. The only

person who awoke as they approached was Sam and he just tipped his finger at Angus like he'd tipped his imaginary hat on his head. A silent acknowledgment.

Once he had her tucked into her bedroll, Angus stroked his knuckles down the side of her face. "See you in the morning, my beautiful bride."

She felt almost giddy. The thrill of being in love.

CHAPTER EIGHT

Angus put on his white dress shirt — or at least something that resembled one. He didn't exactly come prepared with his Sunday best for the Widow Wagon. A white shirt usually had been good enough for a funeral or meeting with someone important in a town. He never in his wildest dreams thought he'd be getting married during one of his journeys though. He saw his job as taking women to their new spouses, protecting them and guiding them until they could find their happily-ever-afters. He'd assumed having one happy marriage would last him a lifetime.

But when confronted with Clara's situation, he had to admit that he'd become very fond of her and the girls. She didn't have the sassiness or bratty behavior of Minnie or Daisy — and he couldn't thank God enough for that. He never minded a little spunk and sassy behavior now and then, but overall, he wanted a woman who willingly submitted. A woman with a little spunk could cause just enough ruckus to ensure that life would never be dull — and it would afford him the opportunity to have a few good discipline sessions. He loved having a woman over his lap. He never *liked* being the cause of her tears, yet he found himself fascinated with how his body responded to them.

He stepped out of the tent. It had be another warm day in Wyoming. This would put them back another day or two, but he couldn't be happier about it. The women had taken it well. He saw a bit of a scowl on Minnie's face, but she'd straightened it up when he directed a raised eyebrow her way.

He walked past the wagon, the women laughing and giggling inside, presumably getting Clara ready for the wedding. He walked toward the gathering of buildings at the trading post. Just past them a small white church had been built for occasions such as this. Apparently, it had become a necessity as a major stop on the Oregon Trail. Between funerals, baptisms, and marriages, the town decided that the preacher needed an appropriate setting for performing such ceremonies.

The church was so new, it still smelled of fresh paint. He climbed up the freshly painted steps, walking into the cool of the church. The preacher stepped down the steps of the altar to meet Angus walking up the aisle.

"Jonas Barnes. It's a beautiful day to get married," the preacher said, greeting him with a handshake. The man's grip was firm, someone who worked the land and didn't just preach. Angus could appreciate that. He liked a hardworking man.

"Angus Warren. I didn't think I'd ever find myself marrying again after my family died. As far as I'm concerned today — the day I marry again — would be a great day even if there was a blizzard or a hailstorm."

"Amen, Angus. Sorry about the family." The preacher clapped him on the shoulder. "How'd you lose 'em?"

"Influenza." Angus wondered how long it would take before he'd be able to say that without tears welling in his eyes. "Clara's a widow too. So both of us are getting a chance at happiness again. Her girls are sweet and I'll be proud to be their father."

"A woman out west without a husband is a bad combination." Jonas shook his head. "I'm glad you found each other on the Widow Wagon. It's a great service that Charles provides, not only for the widows, but also for the men who need a helpmate — or maybe something more — out here in this harsh land."

"Yes, Sir. It's been a help to everyone. I never envisioned benefitting from it myself though. I just thought I was doing a service. But I'm glad."

It was at that moment that Nelly and Rose burst through the door, both girls with daisy garlands and pretty white ribbons in their hair.

"Mister Angus!" They ran down the aisle, and he squatted, scooping up a girl in each arm, kissing their soft necks.

"I'm not sure who these beautiful young ladies are! Do I know you?" Angus furrowed his eyebrows, looking back and forth at the girls as if he'd never seen them before.

"Mister Angus! It's me, Rose. Remember? You buy me candy sticks, the grape ones."

"Rose...hmm, Rose. Oh, you mean Rose *Pickett*? That little girl who's usually running around with dirt on her hands and nose? I remember her. But you, young lady, do *not* look like my Rose."

She scowled at him, her little nose scrunched up. "That's not nice. It's *me*. Should I go and put some dirt on my face?"

"Oh, no! Don't you do that — your ma will skin us both alive," he said, grinning at them. "I know who you girls are, and you both look lovely — like grown women."

"I certainly would skin you alive," a familiar, gentle voice said from the back of the pews. "Don't either of you get dirty though. And don't you encourage them!"

Clara.

She looked like a dream. Daisies weaved through her golden blonde locks, just as the girls had. She had a dress he'd never seen on her before. Nothing fancy, but of pale turquoise color with small white flowers, that made her eyes look as blue as the Wyoming sky. Apparently, she'd brought Sunday clothes along with her too. One of the other women must have had makeup, because Clara's cheeks and lips were painted a pale rosy pink. She looked...stunning.

She'd walked up to him, with all the women of the Widow Wagon and many others filing into the church too, following her up the aisle. Fellow pioneers — and what looked like women from the town not wanting to miss a wedding — began to fill up the empty pews.

Angus grabbed her hand, her soft, silky skin so pale it was almost translucent, and pulled her closer, whispering. "You look like a dream, sweetheart. I can hardly wait to get my hands on you." He kissed her just under her ear, then turned his attention back to the preacher. "Let's do this, Jonas."

Angus wasn't sure how he got through the ceremony; he couldn't keep his eyes off of her and the thought of her skin gleaming by candlelight distracted him mercilessly. Then he felt a small hand slip into his, and he looked down to see Rose beaming up at him, those little dimples showing. He could get lost in those deep blue eyes of Clara's, noting the way the past two months of walking in the sun had brought out a smattering of freckles across the bridge of her nose. She was beautiful, with just a smidgen of adorable — and he couldn't be happier. He startled when a small arm wrapped around his waist, Nelly tucking herself into his side, eyes closed like a contented kitten.

Before he knew it, the ceremony had ended and they were now husband and wife, the preacher beaming at them. "You may kiss the bride."

Angus pulled her to him, her soft lips melding under his as he slowly savored her soft, yielding mouth. They stopped quickly when a chorus of "Ewwwww!" erupted from the girls. Laughing, they all held hands as they left the church, stepping out into the bright, warm July day. A new beginning.

Life had been breathed into what he thought was dead. God couldn't bring back his family, but he'd restored what Angus had lost. He had a wife and two little girls again. He had been devoted and caring the first time around, and would continue to be — but this time he had the added lesson of loss.

Time and people were both fleeting and never guaranteed. It had been a harsh lesson, and not one he'd ever forget.

CHAPTER NINE

The day had been more than she could have imagined. It seemed odd that she had actually contemplated marrying a stranger, but what was a woman to do all alone with two girls? As a schoolteacher, Eugene would have been a good father, but she doubted he could have been as attentive and caring as Angus.

They had played with Angus all afternoon. He'd set up a game of baseball with the kids, finding a long stick and a large ball of yarn from the mercantile. It had been makeshift, but the kids loved it. Soon enough, it became hard to tell who was enjoying themselves more — the little kids or the grown men.

All tuckered out, the women put the children to bed early and quiet descended over the camp. An occasional coyote could be heard in the distance, but rest came early on the plains. The sky was so clear at night. She was certain there had to be a million stars dotting the heavens overhead. A year ago she would never have dreamed she'd find herself halfway across the country, witnessing sights and doing things unheard of in Vincennes, Indiana. More than that though, was the fact that she'd remarried — and feeling happy and excited about the prospect — something she never thought she'd experience ever again.

"C'mon, girl. I've been waiting for this. Time for us adults — finally." He wrapped an arm around her waist, her face flushing hot as she looked up at him through her eyelashes. Though far from being an innocent — she was a widow after all — it still felt strange to think about being naked and doing *that* with anyone other than Matt.

They'd enjoyed sex, she supposed, as much as any other couple she knew. But it hadn't been the focal point of their marriage. It was...necessary. Something you did once a week, like the laundry. She never understood how women at the saloon would do this with strangers — or even other womens' husbands. It didn't seem enjoyable enough to do it for money or pleasure. She wasn't sure she'd ever actually felt pleasure from performing the act.

So, in this new marriage she would continue as planned. She'd close her eyes and just wait until he finished and then roll over and go to sleep. She wondered if she might end up with a baby. He didn't have an empty cradle, so there was a possibility of having a child.

He pulled the flap of the tent back for her, and when she stepped inside she gasped. Nothing prepared her for the work he had done in preparation of the event.

There were lit candles everywhere. Candles in cups, candles on plates, candles in ornate metal holders. A couple oil lanterns had also been lit, lending even more illumination. He'd even suspended a couple candles from the top of the tent. The golden light banished the shadows to the outer edges of the tent, washing everything in a warm, amber glow.

"Angus, this is...just incredible. How did you have time to do this?" She spun around, taking it all in. He'd made a bed on the floor with pillows covered with linens.

"I tried. The hotel manager wanted me to stay at the hotel. But I didn't want to waste money, and I wanted us to start here, the place where we'll be staying each night of our journey. It's our little home away from home." He shrugged, looking around blushing a little. "So, they gave me some linens, blankets and extra pillows to make a bed. The manager said I can keep 'em too so we'll have a bed in this tent."

"It looks nice, Angus." She was at a loss for words as his arms wrapped around her waist, pulling her back to rest against his chest. His hands went to her breasts, fondling them comfortably and naturally. He pushed his hips to her buttocks, his hard cock pressed up against her cleft. She fought the urge to rub against it. He trailed soft kisses up her neck, licking the inside of her ear, her clit sparking into throbbing life. Her breathing increased, her heart beating faster.

He eased her forward a bit. "You have way too many clothes on. Let me get you out of these." His hand expertly began undoing the buttons of her dress, while he pulled the pins out of her hair, letting it cascade over her shoulders.

"It's like spun gold. I love these curls." He pulled on one, letting it spring back as if he was playing with a new toy.

"It's too curly and unruly." She pulled at the locks, tossing them over her shoulder.

"You'll be wearing it down more often. I like seeing those curls running down your back." He pushed her dress over her shoulders, and it dropped in a puddle at her feet. She stepped out of the mound of cotton, pulling it up and placing it gently over the cot to keep it from wrinkling. As soon as she righted herself, he wasted no time unlacing the corset, setting it on top of her dress before pulling her chemise over her head, leaving her standing in nothing but her bloomers. She had one fancy pair, with pale peach and blue ribbons, that she reserved for special occasions — and this was definitely that. Angus cupped one of her cheeks with his large hand and squeezed. Hard. She stiffened in response.

He turned her around to face him. "Those are some

pretty nice bloomers you have on, Mrs. Warren. I'll have to see about getting you some more while we're here."

"Angus. It wouldn't be right for you to get me drawers. What would the other women say?"

"They'd say that I'm a husband who enjoys my wife. I don't give a hoot what those damn women have to say. If I want to buy you nice underthings, then that's just what I'll do. Clear?"

She swallowed. "Yes, Sir."

It'd been a while since she'd been spoiled. If ever. Matt had been kind and generous, but wasn't one for spending on frivolous things like ribbons, candy sticks, and such.

Those large hands that frightened her on more than one occasion came up to cup her breasts, her nipples tightening into stiff peaks under the calluses, the roughness of his skin increasing her arousal. Staring at his large, flat nail beds, the cracks and crevices filled with dirt, made her sex pulse even harder. She loved his hands. So gentle, yet hard. They could stroke lovingly, the knuckles brushing across the sensitive flesh, yet were plenty hard enough to reduce her to sobs when wielded as instruments of discipline.

He leaned forward while the one hand kneaded and massaged her flesh, turning the alabaster skin pink under the roughness and ferocity of his squeezing. He turned her other breast up, taking her deep into his mouth. He sucked on the nipple, the muscles in her womb tightening, making her jerk and moan. He pulled away, leaving her nipple a deep shade of rose now glistening with his saliva, her wet flesh catching the golden flicker of the candlelight. He blew on the moist skin, and she tightened her grip on his shoulders, her hips thrusting in response.

"Oh, darlin', we're going to have some fun here tonight. That feels good, huh?" He sucked the other nipple into his mouth, giving it the same attention. He pulled away, looking at her breasts, licking them both, making sure both of them glistened. He blew on both of them again, the sensation making her clit throb, her heart racing. He slid his hands into her pantaloons, letting the fabric glide effortlessly to the ground.

He stepped back and stared at her, his gaze slowly coursing over her form from her toes to the top of her head, and back down again. "Jesus. You're beautiful."

Uncomfortable at the attention, she put her hand over her pussy, and covered her breasts with the other.

"Nuh-uh," he said. "Now, ya did it. Hands behind your head."

What? I can't put my hands behind my head! My tits will stick right out. It's obscene.

"Darlin', you better do what I say." His voice had dropped an octave, rumbling deep in his chest, a sound she felt more than heard.

Though she knew she should obey him, she couldn't.

"I don't want to." She whined, her voice more like a little girl's than that of a grown woman.

The slaps he landed on her backside sounded like gunshots in the quiet tent, the blows hurting so badly that she found herself dancing up on her tiptoes. He swung her back around to face him again, and she reached back to cup the hot, injured flesh.

"Put your hands. On. Your. Head."

Again, she hesitated.

"Are you looking for a spanking, baby? Is that what you want tonight? Tonight of all nights?"

She shook her head, amazed at how much her bottom hurt.

"Then get your hands on your head before I take the decision away from you and get my paddle." He raised an eyebrow at her, dipping his chin. She knew that look already and decided pushing her tits out wasn't worth the price of disobedience. She laced her fingers behind her head, feeling the bite of the tears behind her lids. It was just so humiliating.

"Oh, darlin', don't cry. I just want to see you without

your hands or arms getting in the way." He tipped her chin up and gently kissed her lips, backing up again to stare at her. He had an obvious bulge in the front of his pants and he whistled low, staring at the tuft of hair between her legs.

Clara had never had anyone look at her this way, not her mother or even the doctor. He stared unabashedly at her, exhibiting no remorse whatsoever for her obvious embarrassment.

"These curls are the color of corn silk." He twirled his forefinger through them lightly, her clit jumping, begging for a rougher touch.

"Oh, Angus!" She couldn't stop herself, her hips thrusting forward.

That low chuckle rolled over her. "You like that, darlin'?"

"Mmmm." She couldn't formulate words to describe how it felt being stroked that way. Matt had done it in the dark — and would be quick about it. She didn't know she could feel like...this. He then slipped his finger inside her.

She gasped. "Oh. Oh my."

"That's right, girl. Checking the temperature. You seem to be just about right — might be time to take a dip."

She should have been offended by that crass statement, but she could hardly breathe, let alone speak. Suddenly unable to even stand on her own, she let go of her head and grabbed his shoulders, her arousal so strong her knees wobbled.

Lord, is this what women mean by swooning?

She thought she might just swoon in Angus' tent tonight.

He scooped her up, walking to the makeshift bed. "You keep your hands above your head. If you bring them down to push me, or cover yourself, I'll be tying them above your head. Clear?"

"Yes, Sir."

What did she just agree to?

Divesting himself of his clothes, he crawled on top of

her, gazing at her all the while. She braced herself, waiting for him to thrust into her and "get this over with." She closed her eyes, mentally preparing, willing herself to endure the coming ordeal with grace.

But instead he trailed small kisses along her chest, focusing on her breasts — again. She looked down at him as he tasted her skin. His hair, the color of coal, had become ruffled, hanging in soft waves about his face. At his temples, gray was just beginning to show, and she couldn't help but touch him there, rubbing the silver locks between her fingertips.

He didn't even pick up his head as he growled at her for her disobedience. She quickly put her hand above her head again. He raised his head up, smiling at her, that small dimple showing in his cheek. "Good girl."

He settled between her legs, his hands sliding under her bottom, cupping a cheek in each hand. What he did next thrilled and mortified her at the same time, his hot mouth settling over her throbbing sex, his tongue slipping between the lips.

Oh my god! Can he put that...there?

"Oh, my God, Angus Warren! What in the name of holy hell do you think you're doing?" She tried sitting up only to feel his heavy hand press against her chest, pushing her back.

"I think I'm getting ready to paddle my new wife." He eased up on his hands and knees, moving closer to her. His cock was stiff and hard, jutting from his body.

"Just who the hell do you think you're talkin' to?" He looked at her hands, now obediently back above her head. "And I warned you about your hands, didn't I?"

She jumped a little when he climbed off her and stood, his member bobbing before him as he walked.

And I thought his hands were big.

Apparently this man was just huge — everywhere. His ass was taut and firm, and her first thought upon laying eyes on it was that she'd like to bite it.

Where in the name of hell did that come from?

She had never bitten Matt's ass, but as she watched the muscles flex as Angus walked, the strong, firm thighs, even the mere sight of him had her hips swiveling.

He walked back toward her with a red handkerchief, the corner of his mouth tilted up. "Whatcha wiggling about, girl?"

"Uhm, I'm not sure." She couldn't keep her gaze off of his cock. She'd never seen one on such blatant display. The amber glow from the candlelight caught the moisture collecting at the head of his member.

He tipped her chin up, forcing her to look at him. "Clara, have you never seen a man up close? It's okay to say you haven't. You wouldn't be the first woman, just married, who ain't ever seen it."

She swallowed hard. He'd given her the ability to save face and admit it without losing any pride.

"No, I've never seen...*that*. It was always dark and under blankets. Are they all that...*big*?"

"You *do* know how to make a man feel good, darlin'. I could lie, but I won't. Yes, most of us are about the same size. Some cocks are bigger, some smaller. You can touch it. It's not going to break." He then tapped his sac. "These, however, are very sensitive. You can touch 'em, but you gotta be gentle. It's like your little button up here." He tapped her clit and she snapped her thighs shut with a strangled moan.

Tentatively, she reached out and just before touching him, looked up at him again, silently seeking approval. He smiled, nodding. She ran her forefinger up his length, circling the head then making her way back down, tracing the large vein on the underside. "It's so soft. How does something that feels like silk become this hard?"

Angus inhaled deeply, closing his eyes, a groan rumbling from deep in his chest.

"Am I hurting you, Angus?"

His eyes fluttered open. "No, darlin'. You aren't

hurting me. It feels so good, I'm…trying to not come."

She blinked back, then grew bolder, taking him in her hand, her grip as firm as she dared. "It's…sturdy."

His laugh only made her more self-conscious, and she let go, looking away.

"Aw hell, I'm not laughing at you, Clara. Yes, it's 'sturdy' — and you're about to find out how sturdy it really is. But first, we're tying your hands above your head because you seem to have a problem listening tonight, and I promised this would happen."

"I'm not sure I'll like that, Angus."

He paused, staring at her for a minute. "It *is* our first night. We have plenty of time to play with tying you up, along with a few other fun things." He tossed the handkerchief to the floor. "You promise to keep your hands above your head?"

"Yes, Sir. I promise." She didn't know that some people considered this 'play'. She just thought of it as a chore, or as other women referred to it, her 'wifely duty.' She'd never heard of women being tied up — and she wasn't sure she wanted to know what that entailed. But so far, she'd been enjoying this much more than she had before.

"Now, I'm going to go back to what I was doing before. I'm going to be licking and sucking your pretty pussy and playing with your little button down there. You keep your hands over your head or you'll not only be tied up, I'll have to spank your little tail too. Clear?"

Did he say suck my…pussy? And play with my 'little button?'

"Angus, is my 'pussy' my privates?"

"You got it, sweetheart. Nothing sweeter in the world — and you'll love it. You'll be begging me to do it again. And soon enough, I'll make you do the same with my cock."

Oh, Lord!

Instead of arguing or denying that any of it might be true, she simply nodded. "Yes, Sir."

"Good girl." He climbed on top of her, situating his hips between her legs, kneading and stroking her breasts. He laved and sucked on her nipples until her womb clenched in response, her pelvis rising off the bed, a slow moan bubbling from her throat, her head tipped back. She gripped the top of the blanket, squeezing it in her fists, her nail beds aching from the strain.

Angus trailed kisses down her belly, kissing her hipbones, paying particular attention to the area just above her quim. Her sex throbbed, and she had the urge to pull his face against it. But she didn't want a spanking, so instead she pressed her feet into the bed, her hips rising, lifting him upon them.

"Feeling a little aroused, girl?"

"Mmmm." She wagged her head, trying to focus on not moving her hands — until he did the next unthinkable thing. He poked his tongue into the curls covering her pussy and licked her button. Before she could restrain herself, she shouted. "Oh, God, Angus! I'm dying!"

Then he stopped. Nothing.

She opened her eyes to see concern on his face. "Clara, sweetie, have you ever had an orgasm or been given release during sex?"

She'd never so much as *heard* of such terms. "I-I don't...I'm not sure. Would I...know?"

"You're absolutely adorable. Yes, trust me, you'd know if you had one — and if you're not sure, then I'm pretty sure the answer is no." He shook his head, and she wondered if that meant he was disappointed. She hadn't even been given a chance. Maybe he'd decided that she wasn't worth it? "You're in for a treat. I'm going to give you your first orgasm."

"I'm sorry I disappointed you. I tend to disappoint people, even when I don't mean to. I'll try to do better, I promise." She felt her lip quiver and she bit it to make it stop.

Now, he'll think you're just some silly crying woman too.

"Disappointed? Is that what you said?" He raked his hand through his hair in frustration. It was one of the signs — along with the tic in his jaw — that let her know when she'd gone too far. "I'm not disappointed at all. I'm amazed that a woman who's been married and has had two children has never been given an *orgasm*. I'm far from disappointed. I'm excited to be your first!" He grinned at her then. "This is like having a virgin bride."

CHAPTER TEN

Angus stared into Clara's moist blue eyes. She had no idea that she had just given him the best wedding present a woman could. An innocent widow — something he would never have expected. He would not condemn Matt — he'd never do that to Clara — but *damn that man.*

How was it possible to have a wife for almost eleven years and *never* give her an orgasm?

That was Matt's loss, and Angus's win. He'd kill himself tonight to make sure that his wife would be screaming with her first orgasm.

"You wipe those tears, right now! I ain't disappointed. Woman, I'm going to have you screaming with pleasure." She looked at him as if he was crazy. "You remember that doubt when your throat is raw. Hands above your head!

He slid his tongue into those golden curls again, swirling it around that already hard little nub, sliding down to her labia, poking his tongue into her, lapping her juices, her body jerking in response. Instead of letting her buck against him though, he placed a hand on each hipbone, holding her still.

She whined in frustration and he laughed against the

soft moist lips of her quim. She'd be taken to the edge and back many times before he'd allow her release. He nibbled and bit his way along those puffy lips back up to her clit, this time sucking on it harshly until her thighs tried closing around his head, then and only then did he release the strength of his suck, pulling back just enough to lightly blow on it.

"Oh! Oh God! Jesus Christ, Angus!" She gasped. "I'm sorry. Oh, I'm –. Oh, Lord!"

"Speechless?" He watched her eyes roll back, arching her back lengthening her neck. She fought against the hold he still had on her hips and her hands let go of the blanket and flexed in the air and went back to the blanket.

Good girl!

He circled the hard, red clit, now released from its hood, the flesh sensitive and taut. He brushed his tongue against it with light, feathery flicks. He let go of her hips and her pelvis jolted upward, forcing him to rise up on his hands to keep contact. He pushed his tongue into her, circling the delicate flesh. Once her hips came back down onto the mattress, he abandoned her pussy completely and started to work small little kisses at the sensitive skin on the inner surface of her hips.

"Oh! Don't stop!"

He laughed. "I told you I'd have you begging."

She glared at him, her eyes narrowed, jaw clenched.

"You might want to fix that attitude. I might not have a paddle, but I hear my hand is much worse."

Her eyes widened and she gave him a nervous little smile.

"That's better."

He kissed and licked each hip until she bucked under his hands once more. ¬He placed his thumb right over her mons, pressing just above her sex. Already prepared, he kept her immobile as she tried to squirm, making him move to push directly on her clit.

"Ooooooooooo, you're making me mad, Angus!" she

said with a growl. He felt his pride swell at that — there was no better sound than making your girl growl during sex.

"Get used to it. You have a lot of years of this," he said, pressing, pushing, and massaging her mons, heightening her arousal to the point that she gasped, her head lolling. It appeared to be time to let his girl finally scream with her release. He could hardly wait. He released her hips, watching them buck and thrust on only air.

Pushing his tongue into her, he lapped up the copious amount of juices waiting for him, then slid up her lips to the swollen clit, lightly flicking and licking, pulling the button into his mouth, sucking on it until she screamed out her release.

Just as he'd predicted.

She writhed and groaned with each tremor, her thighs so tight around his head, he wondered if it would pop right off his shoulders. He continued to lap and suck her until she collapsed in sated, blissful exhaustion.

Sliding up her body, he kissed her neck. "Does your throat hurt, girl?"

"Mmm-hmmm."

"So, did you enjoy your first orgasm, baby?" He pulled one of her soft curls, wrapping it around her face. He loved how silky her hair felt in his fingers, and how the locks sprung back to their original shape, no matter how he played with them.

"Yes…indeed," she murmured.

She still hadn't opened her eyes, so he took her soft, trembling lips in his, working little kisses all over her face, then down her neck, stopping to nip and lick around her collar bone. She moaned and her hips started to rise once more, pressing against him.

Yep, she's gonna be a lot of fun.

He'd enjoy teaching her the ways of a happy marriage.

Lifting himself up, he pushed into her. Her sigh — he forgot how a woman sounded when receiving her husband

— almost made him roar. She wrapped her legs around him, her heels pressed to his buttocks, pulling him into her. He moved slow and easy at first, ramping up her arousal, sliding within her warm, moist sex. When her nails started to dig into his back, he increased the rhythm of his hips, pistoning into her. She squeezed his cock like a vise, straining toward her second orgasm.

"Oh, Angus! Jesus!" She growled, her body stiffening. Then she screamed for the second time with her release, and squeezed him hard, his strangled shout from behind gritted teeth heralding his own orgasm overtaking him. He pounded into her, flooding her with every last drop of his come.

"Jesus, Clara!" He dropped his head into her neck, trying to catch his breath while she lightly stroked his back with those dainty, silken hands, easing him back to reality.

"Do you think you may like having sex with your husband, Mrs. Warren?"

"Lord Jesus, I may never let you drive a wagon again." She opened her eyes. "So this is why women do this for a living?"

She chooses this time to talk about…whores?

"I think there are several other reasons other than that. But, I suppose. I don't want you letting your mind wander that way. Do you understand me?"

He may have created a monster.

"Angus! I'd never in a million years think of that. It's just…it makes more sense now that I know it can be so wonderful."

"I'm just happy you enjoyed it. Now, go to sleep." He gave her a grin. "I'll have you up again soon enough."

CHAPTER ELEVEN

lara woke with a dull ache in her nether regions, a not unpleasant reminder of the active night she'd had with Angus. He'd been relentless, allowing her sleep for an hour or two and then ravishing her body until they would collapse into blissful sleep again.

She sat up, realizing that he wasn't in bed with her. The clanking of tin cups and pots could be heard outside the tent, and the heat in the tent was already stifling. How long had she been sleeping? Could it be that late in the day?

No, the girls would've woken her up by now.

She stood up, feeling the twinge in her quim, the tender tissues swollen from all the attention from her new husband. She found a pitcher of water and a basin, pouring the water into it and using the soap to take a quick bird bath before starting her day.

Angus came into the tent, full of energy and raucous as usual. "You're up. Morning, beautiful!"

"Morning, Angus." Looking over her shoulder, she covered her breasts with the towel.

"What do we have here? Looks like I got here just in time." He winked at her, turning her to face him. "They look neglected. Poor babies." He pouted at her.

"Angus, we don't have time for such foolishness. Besides, aren't you worn out?" She tried pushing him away, but she might as well have tried to move a mountain.

"Don't push me away, woman. I'm playing with my girls." He leaned down, pulling a soft peach-colored nipple into his mouth, her flesh tightening instantly, her hips thrusting in response. She leaned against his thigh, rubbing upon him like a cat in heat.

"God, Angus," she said, sighing, closing her eyes as she tried to steel her willpower, to resist her insatiable need for more. "We have…things to do today besides this."

"We're on our honeymoon — kind of," he said between deep sucking upon her nipples. "The women are watching the girls for us and we have another day before we leave for Soda Springs. So, I can tie you up in here for a whole twenty-four hours before we have to leave."

"Angus! The women will be talking." She tried unsuccessfully again to move him away.

"Angus, Clara? It's Margie." The woman's sweet voice rang out from the other side of the weather-roughened canvas. "I'm taking the girls to the mercantile with me. I need to purchase a few items. I just wanted you to know where they were."

Clara gasped, throwing the towel over her bare breasts. "Thank you, Margie. We'll be over soon."

They both waited until they were sure she had left before daring to speak. "See, Angus? We need to leave this tent. Besides, the girls haven't seen me yet today."

"Relax, sweetheart. No one is talking, and I sat with the girls for breakfast and we played marbles before I came in here to find my sexy wife showing off her wares."

"I was doing no such thing! Lord, you'll have the women thinking I'm some sort of trollop, just like Minnie said."

His hand shot out and swatted her back end so hard — and so loudly — that she had no doubt everyone outside the tent could hear. The skin on her bottom was sore from his frequent attention last night with his slapping and swatting, the blow reigniting the ache in her buttocks.

"You'll never be a trollop, and I won't tolerate you talking about yourself in such a manner." He squeezed her chin between his fingers. "We can turn this into a serious punishment if you don't heed my warning."

"That's…not necessary."

The last thing she wanted was another punishment from this man. Once was enough for her.

"That's my girl." He patted her backside gently. "Get dressed. We'll go see your girls. I'll plunder your body later." He laughed and exited the tent, finally allowing her some privacy.

* * *

A ngus held Clara's hand, much to her chagrin. She still wasn't fully comfortable with being openly affectionate toward him. She'd need to work on that. He liked to hold and touch his woman — often — and she would have no choice but to get used to it.

They walked down the wooden sidewalk that ran along the storefronts of the trading post, saying hello and thanking the passersby for their well wishes. The people of the town were friendly and open, and Angus found himself thinking that it wouldn't be a bad place to start a family. But he had a home in Missouri. He wondered where Clara might want to settle. He'd been to the Oregon Territory many times, and liked it. Perhaps she would decide that the beautiful mountains out West would make a great home.

Just as they neared the mercantile, Margie came rushing down the steps with, dragging Rose behind her. "You just wait until I tell your Ma — and your new pa — what you've done. What were you thinking, Rose? What?"

Letting go of his hand, Clara rushed forward, Angus fast on her heels. "What's going on, Margie?" She scowled at Rose, then looking at Nelly with a questioning glare. "Did one of them do something wrong?"

"Oh, I was just going to find you two." Margie let go of Rose's hand and the little girl ran to her mother, burying her face in her skirts. "Yes. Rose here stole some marbles. I was looking at some ribbons and bonnets, when Nelly came up to me saying Rose took a red marble as well as a couple others."

Angus couldn't believe his ears. The girls had been so well behaved up until now. Rose disappointed him, but children did things like this — and they didn't learn until situations like this arose.

Clara pulled Rose out of the tangle of her skirts, tilting her chin up. "You did what? You know to not take things that aren't yours. What were you thinking, Rose?"

The tears tracked down her cheeks, leaving glistening

trails. "I don't know. The marble was so big and pretty, and we don't have a red one like that. And I knew I didn't have no money to buy it. I'm sorry." Her little lip quivered and she broke into quiet sobs.

Angus knew that this would be part of his new role — husband *and father*. He stepped forward. "I'll handle this, Clara."

"No! This is *my* daughter. I'll handle it." She grabbed Rose's arm, ready to walk away with her.

"I said I'll handle it. I think it will be best if you wait until we've had a little talk." He extricated Rose's arm from Clara's clutches, his wife shooting him a glare that he swore had sparks flying from it. "Girl, I suggest you listen to me on this."

"I'm not sure I want to listen. You've only been a father for twenty-four hours, I know what's best for my children. I don't reckon I like you coming in and taking over like this." Her hands were on her hips now, and passersby were staring.

Something Angus didn't reckon he liked either.

He leaned forward, pulling her close, whispering in her ear. "I'm not taking over. You married me and gave me the right to be your husband — and a father to your children. I've been a father to little girls before. I know how to handle them." He pulled away slightly, but still stood almost nose-to-nose with her. "And I also know how to handle their mother when she acts like a child herself. So, if you want your little tail tanned to a lovely shade of red this evening, you just continue with this little rant you've got going. If not, then I suggest you go sit on a bench somewhere and wait until Rose and I have had our conversation."

Her throat visibly worked to swallow, and although her teeth were still clenched showing her frustration, she nodded her head. "I guess I can sit with Margie over here and wait."

"Good choice. Smart woman." He pecked her on the

cheek, turning his attention to Rose. "Little girl, looks like you and I are having a serious conversation about what you just did. We'll go behind these buildings for some privacy." He scooped her up into his arms, and she buried her head in his neck sobbing.

Angus hated this part of parenting. It broke his heart to hear those little cries, but true remorse and regret only occurred amidst tears. His common sense mind knew this but it was difficult nonetheless hearing her.

As they walked away, he heard Nelly beginning to cry too. "Is he going to paddle her with that paddle, Ma?"

"No!" Clara paused. "Well, I don't think so. I don't rightly know, but Mister Angus will know what to do. Now, Nelly, sit down and stop your dramatics." Thankfully, Rose didn't hear her or she might have become hysterical. He would never use a wooden paddle on a little girl — a young woman or her mother, yes, but never a child.

They rounded the building and just as he suspected, there were some wooden crates in the back. He sat down on one, setting her on his thigh. He used the pad of his thumb to wipe her tears away.

"Are you going to spank me?" Her eyes were big and bright as she peered up at him.

"I'm not sure yet. We know *what* you did. How about you tell me *why* you did it?" He made sure to keep a stern edge to his voice so she'd know he was upset, and how serious he took her misbehavior.

"I just wanted it. It's so pretty. And—"

Angus interrupted her. "Do you have the red marble on you?"

She nodded, tears welling up in her eyes again.

"Let me see it." He held his palm out.

Her small, dainty hand reached into the pocket of her brown-patterned dress. She struggled to fish the marble out, finding it finally and presenting it for him to see. "Ain't it pretty, Mister Angus?"

"It is. It's very pretty — and big." He held it up to the sunlight, letting the ruby-filtered light shine through. "It sure is nice." They each admired it in his hand.

"That's why I took it. It would look nice with the marbles we play with at night. And I wanted it to be mine." She ran her forefinger over the smooth, red glass.

"Miss Margie said that you took more than one." He quirked an eyebrow at her. "Where are the others?"

"I have them." She tapped the pocket of her dress.

"Give them to me."

Her lip quivered. She obviously wasn't used to him being so stern with her, and he fought the urge to pull her against his chest and tell her that he wasn't that angry, just disappointed. But it wouldn't do her any good if he lessened the pain of this lesson.

She pulled out three marbles — yellow, an orange cat's eye, and a lime green cat's eye. "We don't have none like these neither."

"You're right about that. They're all special." He closed his palm over them, putting them in his shirt pocket. "But you know to not steal, right?"

"Yes, Sir."

"But you took them anyway, even though you knew you would be in trouble if you were caught?"

"Yes, Sir." Her little head dropped, her hands twisting in her lap.

"If your pa was still alive, what would happen today?" He tipped her head up, looking into her sad, blue eyes.

"He'd give me a spanking. I'm pretty sure." She wiggled on his leg, squirming at the thought of it.

He nodded, letting the thought of that and a little worry settle into her. "Naughty girls get spankings — most days, anyway. But I think I know of something that'll be worse than a spanking."

Her eyes widened even further.

"I'm going to take you back to the mercantile. You're going to walk up to the owner and tell him what you did, and give him back the marbles you stole. Then you won't be allowed to play marbles for a whole week. You'll have to watch Nelly and I play every night for seven days."

"Oh, no!" She buried her face in his chest and started to cry. She loved playing marbles, even more than Nelly did, the boisterous girl enjoying any reason to be with him and to crawl around in the dirt. This would hurt him more than her though. Her little heart would be broken watching her sister, he had no doubt, but she would never know what a long week it'd be for him too.

He pulled her away, wiping her face with his handkerchief. "There are going to be more times in your life that you'll see things and wish they were yours. You can't just take them because you want them. Sometimes, you just have to wait for it to become yours." He gently rubbed her back, calming her down. "You could've asked me to buy those marbles for you. I'm not saying I would've bought them, but you could've asked. Stealing or taking things that don't belong to you is *never* right. When older people do it, they go to jail. When little girls and boys do it, they get in trouble with their parents. Does that make sense?"

"Yes, Sir."

"I don't want you to *ever* do that again. Next time, I may have to tan your bottom — and you don't want that, do you?" He patted her backside as a warning.

"No, Sir. I don't never want that to happen."

He barely stifled his smile. She was just so damn adorable. Her hair was as bright as the sun, a smattering of freckles decorating her turned-up button nose. She had the same dimple in her cheek as her mother, the sight of it tugging Angus' heartstrings.

"All right. No marbles for a week and you have to confess to the store owner. Once that's all over, you'll be my good girl again." He lowered her on the ground, then stood, fishing the marbles out of his pocket and putting them into her little hand, closing her fingers over the top of them. "Those little marbles don't seem worth all the trouble they caused you today, do they?"

"No, Mister Angus. I wish I'd never taken them." She started to cry all over again. "I can't play marbles all week?"

"No marbles for seven days. It's a long time, but what you did was serious, my girl." He scooped her up, walking back toward the mercantile. Clara and Nelly jumped up, running toward them, putting his hand up, halting them in their steps.

"Not yet. We have some business to attend to with the mercantile owner." He walked up the stairs, still holding her in his arms, putting her down once they entered the store. "You know what to do." He gave her a little nudge in the right direction.

She shuffled up to a counter taller than she was, and she reaching up, carefully setting down the marbles in front of the gentleman. "Sir. I t-took these pretty marbles...I mean, I stole these m-marbles." She looked over at Angus who stood with his arms crossed over his chest, nodding at her to continue. "I'm giving them back, and I'm s-sorry. I won't do it again, I p-promise."

Angus interrupted. "Tell the man what your punishment is going to be, Rose."

"I had to do this, and I won't be able to play marbles for a whole seven days." Her voice broke and she started to cry all over again. Angus strode over to her, lifting her up into his warm embrace.

The store owner nodded. "Seven days is a long time, little one. I'm sorry you did this too. I hope you learned your lesson."

"Yes, Sir." She didn't even pick her head up, still crying into his shoulder as she spoke.

Angus believed in honor and respect. "Look at the man when you speak to him, Rose."

Her head jerked up at the harsh tone. "Yes, Sir. I learned. I'm sorry."

"I'm sure you did. You're forgiven." The man then directed his next comments to Angus. "Thank you for bringing them back, and for doing the right thing. She seems like a very sorry little girl."

Angus shook the man's hand. "She is that, if she's anything."

He walked out and placed Rose into her mother's waiting embrace. She held her close, Rose's arms wrapped tightly around her neck.

Before Clara could ask any questions, Nelly piped up. "Did you use your paddle on Rose?"

"No, Nelly. I didn't paddle her. I didn't even spank her." He rubbed little Rose's back. "Tell your mother what happened."

Her voice sounded so tiny, hiccups interrupting her words now. "I told him I took them c-cuz they were pretty and I wanted them to be m-mine. M-Mister Angus said I would go to jail if I was older."

Damn, the things kids remember.

Clara glared at him, and he couldn't think to do anything but shrug. He had said it — but not to make her worry she'd be thrown in jail at eight years old.

"And th-then he said I had to apologize to the m-man at the store. And then he—" She broke down into little heart-broken sobs, unable to speak another word.

"Angus, what did you do to my child?" Clara swayed with Rose in her arms, trying to soothe her.

"Don't you talk to me like I'm a child, Clara. I took care of this. There ain't nothing wrong with her but being upset about her punishment — as she should be. She stole something." He nodded to Rose. "Tell your mother what your punishment is and stop some of that sobbing. Now."

Rose took a deep breath, her little chest hitching as she tried to swallow some of her sobs. "H-he said that I c-can't play m-marbles for sev-ven days!" She was shouting by the end, dissolving into tears all over again.

God, he forgot how dramatic women could be some

days. He'd meant for it to be upsetting, but he sure didn't mean for her to nearly vomit from crying. And now her mother, who'd be getting paddled instead of her daughter at this rate, was glaring at him *again*.

"Don't you think that's too long, Angus?" She whispered it as if her child had somehow gone deaf from all her crying.

"No. No, I don't. The child needs to find this painful. She stole marbles because she wanted to play with them. The logical punishment is to not allow her to play marbles. It'll make the lesson sink in." He crossed his arms over his chest. "But, if you like, I suppose I could get my paddle and turn her little backside red. Would that be a better solution for you?"

"No! That's not what I meant! I just—" She turned her back to him, and now it was his turn to whisper to her.

"You just what, Mrs. Warren? You want to have that paddle applied to your little ass instead? Because that's where you're headed at this rate. She ain't going to die from lack of playing with marbles, and she needs it to be a painful lesson. And to be perfectly honest, I just don't have the heart to do anything more."

She turned, looking at him relieved that he didn't want to be more strict with her little girl. "I thank you for that, Angus. I wouldn't want you to do anything more either. She'll be fine. It'll be a good punishment. I'm sorry I snapped at you."

"The snapping at me was bad enough, but what has me upset is that you did all of this in front of the girls. We'll be talking about it more later." He lifted Rose out of her mother's arms, putting her on the ground. "That's enough of that, Rose. You're a big girl. Dry your tears and take your punishment."

"Yes, Sir." She wiped her face with the sleeve of her dress.

He took Rose's little hand in his, as he walked down the road with his new family. His wife took his other hand,

and they made their way back to the wagon — and his tent.

CHAPTER TWELVE

L ater in the evening after dinner and the girls had been put to sleep, Angus pulled her into a bear hug, whispering in her ear. "Go inside. Take everything off and stand facing away from the entrance."

"But——" She quickly looked to see if anyone had overheard, her hand going to her throat, her pulse pounding so hard it made her dizzy.

"Now, Clara!" He growled it more than he spoke it, and her feet moved immediately. She entered the tent, feeling anxious and...concerned.

Is this because of my sassiness this morning? In front of the children?

He had said that he'd discuss it later with her, but having heard nothing else all day and everything seeming normal again, she assumed he'd changed his mind and relented. Suddenly, the urge to empty her bladder had become overwhelming. She could go out and ask, but he'd probably see that as trying to avoid her punishment. Better to use the chamber pot than raise his ire any further.

Her knees shook a little as she took her dress and undergarments off. She'd only had one punishment with Angus, and had hoped it'd be the last. Angus could be so

CINCH YOUR SADDLE

sweet, like he'd been with Rose earlier in the day. He'd been stern enough to bring her to tears but once the discussion had ended, things were right back to normal.

That is until evening came around and it was time to play marbles. Nelly and Angus had laid on the ground pulling out the bag and dumping the shiny colored glass balls onto the ground.

"You go first, Nelly."

She'd put her face close to the ground trying to find the best angle to send the blue marble into the pile. She flicked it with her thumb, just as Angus had shown her and when she kicked out some of his marbles, he shouted, "Oh man, Miss Nelly, look what you did? You're gonna pay for that, you know it, right?"

Nelly giggled, rolling onto her back, holding her belly, obviously delighting in Angus's loss.

A little sob from a heartbroken Rose had been heard above the giggles though.

Angus cleared his throat. "Rose Louise, do you need a lesson on how to take your punishment in silence?"

"I don't think so, Sir," she said quietly amidst her continuing sobs. "I'm just...so sad."

"I see that — and hear it too." He looked at Clara, giving her a look that said, 'don't you say a word.' He regarded her in silence a moment longer, then continued, looking back in Rose's direction. "You need to sit quietly and think about *why* you ain't playin' marbles tonight, instead of feeling sorry for yourself. This was your doing, and you need to take responsibility for your choices."

She'd jumped up from the ground, her face scrunched, eyebrows furrowed. "I'm not going to watch, and I don't care that you guys are playing!" She turned to stalk off, not realizing that Angus anticipated her reaction.

He'd grabbed her by the waist, picking her up and walking back to where she'd been sitting, giving her a swat to her bottom and firmly putting her back in her spot. "You *are* going to watch. And you're going to do it quietly

103

and without attitude. If you don't, you'll be sent to bed with another couple swats to change your attitude."

Rose's eyes had been large and tear-filled. Clara felt bad for her but knew to not interfere after her outburst that morning. She'd swallowed loudly, her little chest hitching as she took a deep breath.

"You'll do better to think about how you'll behave in a store next time. It hurts to only be able to watch — I'm sure — but you're a good girl. You can do this." He'd kissed her on the forehead and went back to playing. Rose had sat quietly watching, every once in a while swiping at fresh tears, but overall was able to watch just as she'd been required to do.

When they were done, Angus went over to Rose, scooping her into his arms and sat down, holding her as he whispered and laughed with her for quite a while. He'd stroked her hair, tickled her, and kissed her forehead. Then they both sat quietly while he'd rocked with her, rubbing her back until she fell asleep, her head on his shoulder.

He'd required something that had no doubt seemed out of reach to Rose, but her obedience had been rewarded. As difficult as it must have been not to play marbles, the girl did as required, knowing what the reward was.

And now Clara stood with her bare bottom facing the flap of the tent, hoping he'd use discretion when he came in and not expose her to all the pioneers. The uncertainty of what would be happening had her belly flipping and her clit throbbing. It never made sense to her that her body always reacted sexually to this. Although it wasn't cool outside — quite the opposite in fact — she found herself shivering in nervous anticipation.

It apparently was going to be harder than she thought to relinquish some of the control she had over her life and her children since Matt had passed. She knew Angus once had girls of his own, and knew her girls adored him, but when it came to handing Rose over to Angus and trusting him to do the right thing, it had been downright frightening. And then when she'd come back sobbing, Clara's mind went wild, wondering what he'd done to her child, even though deep down inside she knew he'd been nothing but kindhearted with them.

Now, she'd be paying the price for her overreaction. But he'd understand her reluctance...wouldn't he?

The canvas door whispered open behind her, and she looked over her shoulder, hoping he'd been discreet with exposing her nudity.

"Turn back around, bad girl." He twirled his forefinger in a circle. She quickly faced forward, staring at the dirty, weather-worn canvas again.

"I just don't want everyone to see—"

"I'm not baring your ass to the camp, I promise. Your only concern right now should be to obey what I say. Keep your eyes forward until I give you permission to turn around."

"Yes, Sir." She shuffled on her feet, feeling so unsure with this uncompromising man behind her. She heard the muffled sounds of fabric being moved, things being lightly tossed around. It sounded like he was making their bed. Then she smelled sulfur as matches were lit, the familiar smell of melting candlewax. The tent lit up with the dim light of an oil lantern. She knew he liked to keep it low, preferring the muted light.

Then she heard more movement and a low sigh as he sat down in a chair. *Silence.* The tent had become quiet except for the occasional noise from the camp around them.

"Come here, bad girl." She turned to find him sitting on the only chair in the room. She felt like one of her girls, unsure and small. She shuffled over to him, looking at his hands, thankfully finding no paddle or implement there. She looked around, the room filled with candles. He loved them, and she had to admit that they did lend the room a warm, romantic feel.

He grabbed both her hands, pulling her to stand in

front of him between his knees. "You're going to receive your first spanking as Mrs. Warren. Why are you getting this spanking?"

Well, no need to wonder anymore.

"I yelled at you in front of the kids—"

"And passersby," he added.

She nodded, looking down. "Yes. I'm sorry. And I questioned what you did with Rose."

"Yes, *after* you told me I had 'no right.' And you know better than to question what a punishment is in front of the kids." He raised an eyebrow at her. "I'm betting Matt didn't allow that either."

"No. I was to trust his judgment." She bit her lip, wondering what exactly he intended to do.

"Speak what's on your mind. I see you have something to say."

"I just...it's hard to trust someone new with the kids. I mean, you haven't loved them since the day they were born, and I..." She didn't know how to phrase it any differently.

"That's true. But I've also had the terrible life experience of knowing what it's like to love little girls, and then lose them both. I know how to regret things done and said, probably like no one else — except someone who has also lost a child. I know how to choose my actions and words with care and how to cherish life and love more than the next person." He swiped at the tears that filled his eyes. "I'd never in a million years hurt your child — or anyone's child, for that matter. You gotta trust me on this, Clara. I've come to love those girls, I'd take a bullet or an arrow for those girls without hesitation. Rose's tears just about killed me this morning and again this evening. That's why I cuddled her for so long. I don't want her going to bed feeling neglected or unloved, even for a fraction of a second. Do you believe me?"

How could she not believe him. His heart had been on his sleeve the whole conversation. "I do believe you,

Angus. I'm sorry. I guess I need a lesson on how to obey and submit to my husband."

"I reckon you do." He pulled her to stand on his right side. "I like seeing you like this. Your quim with that fluffy pelt and these beautiful breasts right here at eye level. How perfect."

He leaned close, pulling her soft nipple into his mouth. His eyes closed as he sucked tightly on her, the nipples tightening under the warmth of his tongue. Her clit throbbed and she fought the urge to touch her pussy, hoping he'd stroke it for her instead. He moved to the other breast, nibbling and tugging on the tender flesh, while his hand squeezed the plump globe he'd just abandoned. Unable to restrain her hands, she slipped her fingers between the slick lips of her pussy, circling and sliding in her copious juices.

Angus released her, his lips making a smacking sound. "What do you think you're doing, Clara?"

She extricated her fingers, hiding them behind her. "Uhm...I was...I can't touch myself?"

"Oh, you can touch yourself — if I'm present and if I give you permission. I'd love to watch you come from those long, pretty fingers of yours — but I didn't say you could pleasure yourself. Pleasuring you is my role — and one that I look forward to all day."

He grabbed her hands, holding them up in front of him. He loudly inhaled. "God, I love your scent." He put two of her fingers into his mouth, sucking and licking them loudly. "This is one of the benefits of letting you play with yourself. I get to enjoy your fingers after."

Her face flushed and she feared she might die of embarrassment. "Lord, Angus, you make me so I'll never do it again."

"Oh, you'll do it again, Mrs. Warren. Count on it. I won't have it any other way."

He then tipped her forward over his lap, situating her until he apparently had her just right. His large hand patted her backside, and once again she realized that those hands covered the whole of her bottom.

"When I say that I'll handle something — whether it's with you or the girls — what'll you do?"

"I'll let you handle it, Sir." She clutched his pant leg in her right fist, readying herself.

"Damn straight." He slapped her bottom so hard that her breath rushed from her lungs.

"Oh! Angus!" She stopped just short of telling him that it was too hard, knowing that would probably only reinforce continuing in that mode.

"That's right, little girl, this isn't a fun spanking. You have enough time with those. You'll remember this the next time you open your mouth."

The slaps were crisp and hard, punishing first the left, then the right and then the center of her cheeks. She kept her reactions in check, only gasping here and there, but the heat in her bottom soon grew to be too much to bear, his large, heavy hand impacting the same spot repeatedly. She struggled over his lap, trying to avoid them, and then tried to slip her hand behind her to cover her posterior.

He tucked it onto her back with two punishing slaps to the back of each thigh. "You know better than that, girl." He continued to slap her thighs until she shouted out in pain, bucking her body on his hard thighs.

He tugged her over his left leg, tucking her closer to his body and covering her legs with his right leg. "This'll keep you from moving so much. You're going to learn to not fight me so bad."

"It hurts, Angus!" And on those words, her voice broke and the flood gates opened.

"Good, means I'm doing my job well." He stopped spanking and rubbed her very sore bottom with his callused hands.

"Ow. Do you have to rub it?" His roughened skin didn't feel like it was soothing the injured flesh, instead it felt like sandpaper.

"Yes, I do as a matter of fact. I love the feel of this hot red ass under my palm and I love feeling the scorched flesh being squeezed in my hands. I love your ass, Mrs. Warren." He continued to plump her bottom, his fingers sliding between her cheeks, delving into her moist pussy. Angus pushed a couple fingers into her, pumping her channel, the wet sounds filling the tent.

"Lord, Clara, maybe I should just take my cock out and have you ride me in this chair." He let his thumb stroke her clit and she about shot off into her orgasm, stiffening over his lap until he pulled out. "Uh-uh, you're not coming yet. Let me finish this spanking, and then we'll see about both of us finding our release."

He then proceeded to slap her bottom with such a vigor, that she had no doubt that every pioneer in the area heard her screeching. The force pushing her forward over his thigh, shaking and bouncing her breasts off each other and his thigh. It felt at some point like she'd gone numb, her bottom and mind were just one big source of pain. Thankfully the last harsh volley of slaps ended almost as quickly as it started and she'd been left to sob pitifully. He released her hand and she tried wiping her face staring at the puddle of mud her tears had made mixed with the dusty, dirt floor.

His low rumbling comforted her although she couldn't discern what he'd been saying to her.

"Oh, Angus. I'm so sore and so sorry." She sobbed into his leg.

"I'm sure you are. I'm sorry you're so sore, girlie. You'll do better next time, I have no doubt." She felt him rustling next to her left hip, not giving it any mind, until she felt something warm, bobbing off against her left hip. She looked over her shoulder to see his large cock, stiff and twitching, fluid leaking from the slit.

"C'mon, girl, how about we both find our release? Spanking your ass has me completely worked up and by the beautiful shine on your quim, you ain't doin' so bad yourself."

"Angus! Dear Lord, do you have to be so crass? What would the preacher say if he heard what you just said?"

Angus laughed at her. "Clara, I reckon he'd be blinking like a frog in a hail storm, and I really don't give a shit either." He helped her up, guiding her to slide down onto his stiff cock.

"It's just like riding. I'll guide you. Feel free to use your hands on your clit to help you come, girl."

Her toes touched the floor and she rode up and down on him, the friction of his cock rubbing on her clit. He cupped a cheek of her ass in each hand and again the calluses rasping on her sore flesh, but this time instead of being uncomfortable, it heightened her arousal.

Each time he'd squeeze and lift, her sex flexed and throbbed in response. "Jesus, Clara. You're so damn tight, squeezing me." She levered up higher, thrusting down on his cock, hard, pounding her flesh. The rhythm increased in pace and strength until they both shouted with their release, Clara dropping her forehead onto his shoulder.

They stayed in position, catching their breath. Angus slowly started to stroke her back. "Clara? Sweetie? You awake?"

"Mmmm." She couldn't even figure out how to respond with real human words.

"Let me get you on the bed. I wanna play with you tonight, and you're in the right frame of mind for it too." He picked her up, letting his semi-erect cock slip out, then picked her up, cradling her in his arms. He gently placed her onto her front. "I'm going to pull your hair up and out of the way, and then we'll get started."

Started? Started on what?

CHAPTER THIRTEEN

He piled her hair up on the top of her head, wrapping it in a loose bun, keeping it off her back. "Stay on your belly." He ran his hand over her hot, red bottom, his fingers gently testing the ridged welts. "You have a pretty sore little backside, don't you, girlie?"

"Yes, Sir."

She squirmed under his touch. "I think I'd behave for a while if I were you. This will be sore tomorrow." He squeezed and pinched her ass, filling his hands with the plump, soft flesh.

"I'm going to pour some warm wax onto your body."

Her head swiveled, the large eyes not even blinking. "You're going to do...*what?*"

"Trust me, Clara. You'll like this. I'm not going to hurt you. I've done it before. It's very relaxing and sensual." He carefully took a wet washcloth and wiped her back and freshly spanked bottom.

"Mmmm." She squirmed, lifting her hips. He obliged her, sliding his hand down, cupping her pussy, her juices coating his palm. Angus slipped a finger into her, rubbing her special spot until a low growl rose from her chest.

"My girl seems ready for more play already." He kissed her reddened cheeks, the warmth of her punished flesh upon his lips making his cock jerk to attention. "We'll start with your back, and shoulders."

He held up the candles in front of her. He'd chosen a yellow, red, and black tapered paraffin candle. "These are paraffin wax, much more gentle than beeswax. It won't sting as much and you'll just feel a nice soothing warmth as it runs down your back and spine. The yellow feels cool to the skin, and the red and black feel hotter."

She still wasn't sure about this. Candles were hot — and they burned! She'd warned the kids about them for years, but she promised him she'd trust and obey, and after her spanking and the sex, she wasn't exactly sure she had the energy required to tangle with Angus again.

"Raise up, I want to put this pillow under your hips." He lifted her pelvis until her bottom felt as if it had been elevated to an obscene height, all of her treasures on blatant display. "Now, close your eyes. I just want you to feel."

She looked one last time as he held up two yellow candles, one in each hand, about four feet over her back. At the quirk of his brow, she quickly closed her eyes, her heart racing in anticipation.

The first drop felt cool upon impact, but as it slid down her spine, the trail left a warm glow in its wake. The drips fell consistently and almost in a rhythm, moving and gliding down the length of her spine. The drops started just above her bottom, gliding to the small of her back. She felt a few drops fall onto her buttocks, but they didn't feel as cool hitting her spanked flesh, but rather they were almost...comforting. Her hips jerked and she gasped.

Should I move? Will it make him to burn me?

"You're fine, girl. You can move — it's meant to be arousing. So, if you feel like grinding yourself on that pillow, you just go ahead. As a matter of fact, I kinda recommend it." He chuckled above her.

The hot fluid continued to slide down her ass to the small of her back, with random drips upon her bottom every time her hips were unable to stay still. Her clit rubbed on the cotton fabric of the pillow, her flexing hips pressing into the pillow, seeking her release.

"Remember, you aren't allowed to come until I give you permission. Rub all you want, but don't bring yourself to completion." He had an edge to his voice that brooked no disobedience.

"Did I know that rule? I'm not sure I knew that rule?" She peeked an eye at him.

"You do now. See that you heed it." He nodded at her before putting the yellow candles in their holders, picking up their red and black counterparts.

"Close your eyes." He dripped the wax over her shoulder blades, running over her ribcage. Warm. Warmer than the yellow. The fluid fell in hot rivulets until her rib cage felt completely warmed and relaxed.

Then the wax cascaded onto her bottom in random patterns, the heat right on the edge of uncomfortable, drawing a gasp from her.

"It burns landing on that naughty backside, doesn't it?"

"Yes, Sir." She moaned, wiggling in response. "I'm not sure I like it."

"We won't stay there for long...this time."

What did he mean by that?

He moved up her spine, leaving a nice, warm trail of wax settling into her back. She couldn't remember the last time she felt this relaxed. She lay there, reveling and relaxing into the wax, eyes closed as the world melted away, only warm versus hot versus cold permeating her consciousness.

"C'mon, girl." He sat her up on the bed, letting her catch her bearings. He knelt behind her. "Now, I'm going to take this wax off of you. I'll be using the dull side of my knife to separate it from your skin. We'll go slow, so it doesn't hurt or become uncomfortable." The blade was cold against her warm skin as the wax was removed. It tugged, but wasn't painful. The quiet process of peeling it off helped her come back to reality.

"What time is it, Angus?" She had no sense of how long they'd been playing with the wax. For the first time in years, she'd been lost in something that didn't entail cleaning, cooking, or family. And she didn't feel guilty about it either; it had been such a calming process.

"It's about eleven o'clock at night." He slowly pulled off a sheet of wax that covered most of her upper back. He showed her the large piece, and she took it from his grasp.

"Oh, Angus. I'm not sure I want to throw this away. I loved this, and I can't believe it's that late. How long did we do this?"

"That's the whole point. It's soothing for you — and for me. I loved watching you in that light slumber, relaxed under my wax painting." He continued to pull off more of the sticky stuff. "Lie on your belly. I need to get this all off your bottom."

She rolled over onto her tummy, still feeling embarrassed to be so exposed to him even after everything they'd done. The knife didn't feel as comfortable on her sore flesh and the tugging on the skin hurt much more where she'd been punished. "Ow! That kinda hurts...*there*."

"That's why I didn't let much wax settle there. Misbehave again, and there is always a risk that I'll wax your bottom as a whole. Of course, I'll stay away from your anus and your sex, but having hot wax dripped on a freshly spanked ass and then scraped off, is a punishment all in itself. Keep it in mind, girl."

"Yes, Sir."

She didn't even want to think about how much such a punishment would hurt.

CHAPTER FOURTEEN

S he was relieved that she didn't have to wake to the women grumbling and had a husband to wake up beside her. Nelly and Rose stayed in the wagon as they had been, Angus insisting from day one that they sleep off the ground and in the safety of the wagon.

And to keep the grumbling and gossip down — even though the women of the Widow Wagon seemed happy for Clara and Angus— Clara made sure to be up in time to assist with the morning chores and normal routines. Today, it was her job to cook breakfast with Sam. She started a large pot of corn porridge while Margie cooked the bacon and Sam made Johnnycakes. After a couple months of this, they had quite a system going and the women could literally do it while still half asleep.

Meanwhile, Minnie and Lizzie had been rolling up the bedding, loading it in the wagon. It would be their job to wash the dishes after breakfast was over. The women had been seeking Angus out to escort them on the walk out to do their morning business. Sometimes, they went as a group and other mornings they just went out in pairs.

"I'm telling you I ain't doin' it. I'm got my womanly, and I'm not getting him or you to come with me just so I

115

can relieve my bladder. It's just embarrassing and there hasn't been a damn thing that's happened here since he warned us."

Minnie.

Of course, it was Minnie bucking at the rules again. She'd been struggling with his strict orders since he'd instituted them.

Clara couldn't keep her mouth shut. "Minnie, you know as well as I do that there were Indians just the other day. And if I recall — which I'm sure you can too — you got your ass paddled for it. So, if I were you, I'd just swallow my pride and go do your business with Angus nearby for protection."

"Of course, that's your response. I wouldn't expect you to say anything less. You're his wife now. You must obey his rules. I don't have to, and I'm gonna do what I want." Minnie scanned the campsite, obviously looking for Angus. "While he's gone rustling up the cattle and oxen, you women cover for me. He won't even know I'm gone."

Minnie hiked up her skirts, running toward the area they used for times such as these. Clara hated this; she knew that Minnie put herself at risk doing this with renegades and Indians around. They'd been told that East of Soda Springs the renegades were the biggest issue, west of Soda Springs the Shoshone were the issue.

She stopped cooking, looking over at Margie. "Should I follow her anyway? Angus will be cross — and he may be pissed at me for not saying something."

Margie wiped her hands on her apron. "As I see it, she's a grown woman — and one with a sore ass to boot. If she chooses to disobey, it isn't my problem. And furthermore, it isn't up to me to tell on her."

Clara nodded. There was logic in that. Minnie made her own decisions, even when Clara tried to tell her not to. She'd done all she could.

Angus ambled up to them, swiping a piece of hot bacon out of the pan. "How's it going this morning?"

They exchanged looks, wondering how they should respond. Clara spoke up first. "Good. Everything is good."

"Why do y'all seem a little off today?" His keen gaze scanned them as he spoke.

Damn him!

"What do you mean? We're tired, Angus. It's early." Clara said it with enough attitude that his eyes narrowed at her.

He then sighed. "Yeah, it is early. I'm tired too."

"Wait...where?" He spun in a circle and Clara's heart started to beat so fast she found it hard to swallow. "Where's Minnie?"

Clara and the women stood, none of them speaking a word, staring at him, hoping he'd just forget — or become distracted.

And distracted is what they all became.

"Help! No! Put me down. Put me down now! Help!" Minnie screamed in the distance. Everyone dropped what they were doing, running instinctively toward her cries. The men first shouted for the women to get in the wagons, then grabbed their weapons and charged toward the direction of Minnie's distress.

Clara dove for her girls, rushing them into their own wagon. Peeking out of the back, it appeared that there were four unidentified cowboys on horses, and Minnie, her green dress fluttering in the wind, could be seen flailing and screaming, thrown onto her belly over one of the horses.

Angus and the other men shot at the outlaws, hoping to stop even one of them. Several of the men ran to their own horses, apparently intent on trying to catch up to the bandits, if only to rescue Minnie.

But all too soon, the outlaws made their escape with Minnie. She'd been kidnapped by a bunch of renegades!

* * *

Angus and the men called the women out of the wagons, telling them that it was safe now. They had some of the older girls to take the children to play a safe distance while they interrogated the pioneers.

The women in the Widow Wagon had been evasive when he asked where Minnie was, and they seemed downright skittish before that. Now he knew why, and he'd just have to find out what they knew — and why they didn't say anything.

"I know there's a lot of you gathered here today and many of you weren't even traveling in Minnie's wagon. But we want to know anything you saw this morning." He paced slowly in front of all them, making eye contact with each one. "I want you to tell us any details, anything that didn't seem right. If you saw her this morning, when you saw her, where she was, and if you saw anything in the distance. These are important facts if we're going to get her back."

As suspected, it was his women who couldn't keep eye contact — *at all.*

"I'm going to address those of you from other wagons first. Did any of ya see her this morning? Raise your hands if you did."

Only two raised their hands.

"The rest of you are dismissed. You can go back to fixing breakfast and doing bedrolls. We'll call you back if we need to." He walked up to the two women who had admitted to seeing Minnie.

"Where and when did you see Minnie this morning?"

The first woman, if you could call her that, appeared to be no more than fifteen — and frightened as hell. Her eyes were large, and her hands shook.

"Baby, it's all right," Angus said. "You ain't in trouble, okay?"

He rubbed his hand down her arm. "I'm just asking questions. You wanna help us find her, right?"

"Yes, S-sir."

"When did you see her?"

"She was doing the b-bedrolls, and I heard her t-talking to the women." She wrung her hands in front of her. Angus felt bad for her, the young girl obviously afraid either of the situation or him — or both.

"Did you hear her say anything that would help us find her?"

"No, S-sir. I swear I didn't see anything but that."

"There, you're done. You did fine, sweetie. You can go back to doing what you were doing before the commotion." He watched her go.

Then he addressed the second woman. At first glance, she seemed young, but the laugh lines at the edges of her eyes indicated she was probably closer to thirty five than twenty five. Or was it that Angus, the closer he got to forty, thought everyone seemed young now.

"So, you say you saw Minnie this morning?"

"Yes, Sir." She glanced at the women of the Widow Wagon. He stole a look his shoulder to see their reactions. Again, avoiding eye contact at all costs, they all became suddenly very interested in the ground in front of them.

Yep, they're hiding something.

"Tell me what you saw."

"I saw her leaving toward the area where...where we do our business. But she was alone." The woman's eyes widened, no doubt knowing the rules were strict for *all* the wagons, not just his wagon. No woman or child was to be anywhere alone. Ever.

Angus had just assumed that one of the women went with Minnie even if it wasn't from his wagon — although the rules were that she was to ask permission first. But, he didn't think she'd broken two rules. Even Minnie didn't seem quite that brazen.

Now, he needed to figure out if the women of his wagon knew about any of this.

"Are you sure no one was with her?" He tilted his head, curious to see what her answer would be.

"Yes, Sir. She'd been arguing with the women of your wagon first, and then she stormed off." She did a quick glance out of the corner of her eye toward the Widow Wagon women.

"Don't you worry none about my women. They'll behave. You only answered questions truthfully, and I appreciate it. You can go back to your chores." After she'd made it back to her site, he turned, hands on his hips as he walked back to his women.

"So are all of you in agreement that Minnie stormed off alone to do her morning business?" The women were all still looking at the ground. "Eyes on me. Now." All of them looked up, reluctantly making eye contact.

"Yes, Sir," they murmured, almost in unison.

He sighed. They'd been told many times that under *no* circumstances was a woman to be alone. They were to find a man and tell him — or go with her, regardless of whether or not she wanted a companion."

"So, who was she arguing with before she stormed off?" None of the women responded. "Lizzie, who was she arguing with?" Lizzie seemed to be the only one on this wagon that had a mild spirit. She didn't argue, and did as she was instructed with very little or no complaining. He'd get an honest answer from her.

"Uhm..." Her eyes flicked toward Clara. He quirked an eyebrow at her and she swallowed hard. "Clara, Sir."

In two strides, he stood in front of his new wife. "Is that so, Mrs. Warren?"

"Yes, Sir." Her eyes instantly filled with tears.

"And you didn't think to tell me that when I came back to the site?" He grabbed her chin between his thumb and forefinger, leaning in closer. "Or to tell one of the other wagon masters? Or, how about this, to follow her *anyway*?"

"No, Sir. I guess not...I guess I..." She closed her eyes unable to drop her gaze.

"You guess not." He dropped his hand from her face, letting out an exasperated sigh. "We've discussed this. All of you. Over and over again."

He needed to figure out where Minnie had been taken. He hadn't lost a woman yet, and he wasn't going to this time either. But first it was essential that he got his emotions under control.

"So none of you women — *none of ya* — took the time to follow her or do anything to ensure her safety? We'll be delayed for a few days here. The Sheriff is gathering a posse of men to find her and catch these renegades. They've taken captives before, and they usually just want money to bring the woman back. But this time, they say they're going after them."

He couldn't delay their journey too much longer or they'd risk being in the snow before they made it to Oregon country. He couldn't risk the lives of his new wife and children, nor any of the other women in order to save one. As much as he wanted to find Minnie, it wouldn't be worth waiting too long. They'd wait three, maybe four days before leaving — and after that he'd just have to deal with the failure and loss.

"I should paddle every single one of your asses. But I'm not going to. I think the guilt of her being taken is punishment enough." He waved his hands at them. "You all go back to your chores."

They started to disperse, but he grabbed Clara's arm, whispering in her ear. "You, however, will be getting your tail tanned later. Think on that for the rest of the day." He turned on his heel, leaving her standing there. He needed to talk to the other men and let them know Minnie had been left alone.

Then he needed to calm himself down before tending to his disobedient wife.

CHAPTER FIFTEEN

Minnie just knew she'd vomit. She'd been thrown over the horse and the saddle horn was jammed painfully into her belly. Every time she tried to break free and throw herself off the horse, the vile man riding the beast would swat her backside so hard she bit off a scream.

"Stay still. You ain't getting off this horse until I say, and if I gotta stop to make that point clearer, it'll be said with my hand on your bare backside. So stop your kicking and flailing." He swatted her backside several times in a row until she screeched.

He had long brown hair, and a beard. She couldn't see much of him in this position, but none of them seemed too appealing. Only God knew how long it'd been since any of them had showered. The only thing she was sure of was the strength and hardness of his right hand. After several of those painful smacks, she decided that she'd lay low for a bit and escape *after* she got off the horse.

"You're gonna be a sorry girl. We ain't letting you back to those people until they pay us a good sum to get you back. How much trouble were you? 'Cause if they're glad to be done with you, you'll be sold off at the closest saloon."

The rider who spoke to her had ridden up to their left. He appeared to be as dirty and unshaven as her captor. She didn't want to think about the fact that Angus might be glad to have her gone. What if he decided to not pay for her release? She couldn't be a whore. She'd been bred for better than a common trollop in a saloon.

Smack! "Ow!" She tried to reach around to rub her sore bottom, but his body was in the way.

"Kane asked you a question. How much trouble were you out there? And who were you with?"

The vile man they called Silas, her captor, kept a hand on her ass, she assumed as a warning. "Uhm. Well, I was a little bit of trouble. But the Widow Wagon will come looking for you all. Angus ain't going to let anything happen to one of his women."

At that, Kane laughed, yelling over his shoulder. "Red, get your ass up here. You ain't gonna believe this."

The last one of the renegades had red hair, which she assumed was the source of his name. He had a couple teeth missing, and she didn't like the evil sneer he shot her way, like she was a fresh piece of meat hanging from a tree.

Kane let go an annoying laugh — which seemed never ending — then pointed at Minnie. "She says she's from something called the 'Widow Wagon' and was, as she put it, 'a little bit of trouble.'"

"What the fuck is a widow wagon?" He looked to Silas to see if he knew. Silas shrugged and gave him a smile. "I ain't never heard of it neither, so don't ask me." At least Silas had all his teeth, and although his hair and beard were long, he seemed to be a little better groomed. Not that any of them were a prize.

"Speak up, bitch. What the fuck is a widow wagon? And what the fuck is your goddamn name anyhow?" Red pulled on her hair, forcing her head up to look at him.

Although the tug burned her scalp, she shouted and

spit out the words, "It's a wagon for women who've been widowed that brings them to new spouses…it's a mail order bride service. My name is Minnie."

Kane sat staring at her in amazement. "Well, I'll be goddamned! Who knew such a thing existed. You boys ever hear of such a thing?"

They both murmured that they hadn't. "So, you were some trouble, Minnie? I can see that. You cause trouble here, we'll tan your ass — or worse. If they don't want her back, we'll just have to leave her at one of the saloons. They'll take her. She's pretty and she isn't a virgin since she's a widow. So, that'd be a plus."

Good lord, they were talking about her like she wasn't even there. She'd have to make sure she behaved until Angus could find her.

He'll come to find me, won't he?

She'd more than likely have to pay for taking a risk with her life, especially after she'd been explicitly warned. Minnie knew she'd take whatever punishment Angus deemed necessary. Anything to get away from these men. They couldn't be that far from Angus. They'd only been riding for a bit. If she bit Silas's leg, she'd more than likely be able to get away and hide among the rocks in the distance.

She'd just have to run like hell to those rocks and hope they didn't ride her down like a dog.

Minnie adjusted herself so she'd be able to bite the inside of his thigh just above the knee. She opened her mouth and bit as hard as she was able, but didn't take into account how thick his pants were. By the level of his shouts and swearing, she had more of an effect than she thought. She also didn't take into account how awful his pants tasted. Sweat, dirt, and god knew what else.

"Jesus Christ, get your fucking teeth off of me!" He yanked on her hair, but she grit her teeth and bit down even harder. She swore she tasted blood.

Then she felt Red behind her tugging on her dress. She

had to let go and escape. If she didn't, she'd lose her chance — or Red would grab her. And for some reason, being with Silas seemed like the lesser of two evils.

She loosened her jaws and pushed off his thighs, falling into a heap on the ground, the air knocked out of her when she hit the hard dirt with bone-crunching force. She struggled to get up, finding her footing and then running like her life depended on it — which it did. The clomp of hooves pounded behind her and they probably would have caught her, except someone flattened her to the ground, knocking the wind out of her for the second time.

"You just made a grave mistake, missy. You'll be paying for it with your hide too." She tried flipping onto her back — to no avail. He straddled her backside, but now held her down with a firm hand in the middle of her back, his other hand rucking up her skirts.

Oh, God! Is he going to violate me? Here in the wilderness?

"I'm sorry! I'm sorry!" The panic rose in her chest, making it hard to breathe and she felt like she might swoon, like her mama did when stressed.

"Not as sorry as you're going to be, little girl. I'm going to tear up your ass. I'm bleeding down my leg from your teeth!"

He continued pushing up the heavy layers of her skirts, then proceeded to pull her pantaloons down. Now the fight was on! She'd be damned if she'd be laid bare to not only God and Country but to these damned lowlife outlaws.

She started to buck and writhe her hips, kicking her legs, trying to get traction and flip over to make her escape once more.

"Ooooo wheel! She's puttin' on quite a show ain't she, Red!" Kane's voice was somewhere behind her, along with Red's. She stilled her legs, closing them to hide herself from their view.

"Too late for that, girl. We seen that pretty little pussy. Might as well keep them open so we can enjoy the view while Silas whips your hind end!" Red's laugh was deep, and evil, the mere sound of it enough to make her stomach roil.

"Why don't you assholes shut the fuck up, so I can concentrate on giving her the licking she deserves? Don't you have something better to do?" Silas climbed back onto her legs, and although the restraint made her anxiety rise as she wondered what he would do next, she hoped that he had effectively blocked the view of her quim from those vile men.

"Well, hell! I guess we got nothing else to do, but since you're sitting there, we can't see none of her charms no how." Red spit onto the ground. She should've known he chewed. It explained why his teeth were such a mess.

"We'll stay here. Nothing else to do, and I can't think of anything I'd rather do than watch a woman's ass being turned red by a belt."

A belt?

"Just keep your yaps shut! I'm pissed enough without your yammering!" Silas pushed her pantaloons further down her legs and the air whispered across the juices gathered along her puffy lips.

The line of fire that lashed across her cheeks had her shouting and reaching back to stop it at all costs. He used a single huge hand to pin both of hers at the small of her back.

"And now your punishment begins, Minnie. Your ass will start to tingle the next time you even *think* of biting." He set out with a vengeance with the belt, strike after strike hitting her bottom. Minnie couldn't remember the last time she blubbered like a child. She screeched, screamed and sobbed into the brown dirt, clawing her fingers into it, hoping to drag herself away from him.

Then he stopped. It was over and she felt a moment of relief amidst her agony. She'd survived and swore she'd never bite another soul for as long as she lived. Her sobbing and incoherent apologies continued until she'd had some time to catch her breath.

The next words turned her blood cold. "Now, we'll start teaching you a lesson you won't forget, girl. Teeth are not for skin. They're only for food. When I'm done whipping your bottom, you'll repeat those words to me. Say them out loud now, so I know you're listening."

She hesitated — apparently too long. The belt hit her thighs and one long wail tore from her throat.

"Say it!"

"T-teeth are not for skin. They're only for food. I'm sorry!" She looked over her shoulder at him, and she thought she saw something cross his face. Remorse? Pity? She didn't have time to think any longer about it because he lifted his arm again, and that black snake of a belt hit her ass with such a flurry of lashes that she wondered if he'd ever stop. She wasn't sure she'd ever felt pain like this.

She could think of nothing else but getting away from the all-consuming pain overtaking her. Her body was stiff and taut, every muscle in her legs, bottom, and spine constricting. And at just about the time when she realized she may lose control of her bladder, he stopped.

Her screams kept rising from her sore, dry throat. She wondered how much dirt she'd sucked into her mouth. He seemed to be breathing as deeply as she.

"What lesson did you learn, girl?" Silas kept his hand on her backside as a warning.

She struggled to catch her breath and find her voice. " T-Teeth are n-not for skin. They're only f-for food."

She broke down into pitiful sobs, her chest constricting.

"Jesus, Silas." Kane whistled. "She really pissed you off, I ain't ever seen you this upset. She won't be sittin' on a horse for a few days with that ass."

"No, shit! That was some ass whoopin' you just doled out." Red laughed.

"Why don't you assholes give us some time here, so I

can get her situated and sorted out before we leave again." The disgust in his voice surprised her. Even after what he'd just done to her, she still felt better about him than she did Red, a man who seemed utterly devoid of conscience or empathy.

Red snorted. "Pffft. When did you become a girly girl? Christ, just pull her damn drawers up or rip them off of her and let's get goin'."

"Why don't you idiots fuck off. Give us a few minutes. She ain't ready to go yet and I ain't discussin' it further. If you want I can fight both of ya." He stood up, the belt still dangling from his hand, straddling her naked body on the ground.

"C'mon, Red. Let's just let him be. He's all riled up. It isn't worth it." She heard the horses' hooves as they left.

Silas' hand rubbed lightly over her bottom, fingertips pressing at various spots upon her flesh. She flinched at the tenderness in some areas.

"What in the name of hell possessed you to bite my leg? Jesus, I hate that I did this to your ass, but at the same time you deserved every damn lick I gave you." He pulled her drawers up, and she felt mortified, like a small child having Daddy pull her pants up after a spanking. Her chest hitched when she took a deep breath, a side effect of crying so hard.

He pulled her dress down, gently grabbing her by the elbow. "C'mon over here. Let's get you sorted out before we have to leave again." He tugged her into his lap, tucking her head against his chest. "Damn stubborn, naughty girl. Bet you won't bite anyone again, will you?"

"No, Sir. Ever."

"I don't imagine you will. You need to do as you're told, especially now. Red and Kane won't tolerate you causing trouble, trust me on this." His voice rumbled over her, her ear against his chest registering it as a deep rumble.

She pulled away, looking up at him. "What about you?

You don't seem to be the patient sort either."

She suddenly realized what she'd said to the man who had just punished her ass like none other in her lifetime.

He laughed. "No, I don't suppose you see me as a patient man, do you?"

She shook her head. "Are you going to...have your way with me?"

"No! Hell no! But promise me you'll listen and do everything I tell you to — the first time."

Why did she feel like she could trust him? With everything he'd just done to her, she should be figuring out how to put a knife between his eyes. Instead, she nodded. "Yes, Sir. I promise."

He pushed her hair behind her ear, wiping tears off her face. "Good girl. Now, let's get you up on the horse." He stood with her, walking her back to his horse. She couldn't stand the thought of sitting on his lap or on the saddle. She just couldn't.

"Silas, I don't think I can sit." Her eyes filled with tears again. How'd she end up in this situation, begging for mercy? Disobedience and stubbornness.

She'd been the cause of all this trouble.

"Oh, I agree. You won't be sitting on that little tail for a while. You'll be lying over my lap until we get to Independence Rock. That way if you don't mind, I can reignite the fire there." He winked at her and before she could catch herself, she scowled at him.

He quirked an eyebrow at her. "Do you think that's wise, little girl?"

She swallowed. She'd done it again. She'd really have to rein herself in. "No, Sir. Sorry."

"I guess I'll be lenient. I'm sure the thought of being spanked even over all these skirts probably sounds pretty awful at this point." He sat up on the horse, reaching down for her. He pulled her up as if she weighed virtually nothing, easing her over his lap. "You comfortable?"

"What're you doin' asking if she's comfortable? Have

you gone sweet on her, Silas?" Red spat his words at Silas.

"So what if I am? You did with Annie!" Silas bit out his answer with as much attitude as Red had.

Minnie lifted her head, seeing Red's eyes narrow. *Hair trigger.* It was a phrase her father had for hotheaded boys, and that was all she could think when she watched his reactions to things. She needed to handle him with extreme caution.

"That I did. Are you fucking her tonight and making her yours?" Red stared at her. She swore she felt like she was naked over Silas' horse.

"Probably. But if I fuck her, or don't fuck her, it's none of your business. I'll do as I please with her and then we'll get the money we need by dumping her back at the Widow Wagon." She looked over her shoulder at Silas. He'd said he wouldn't violate her. But when their eyes met, his jaw clenched and he shook his head infinitesimally. She dropped her head. Did that mean he wouldn't? Or did that mean, don't argue about it he'd do as he wanted? Would he actually defile her? Did he even care that it would ruin her?

They're renegade outlaws — they don't give a damn about your reputation.

Regardless, she knew better than to say a word. If he wanted her to keep her mouth shut, shut it would stay — at least until her bottom healed and the throbbing subsided.

CHAPTER SIXTEEN

She closed her eyes as his forefinger slide through her slick lips, her pussy dripping in anticipation and nervousness. Clara had never seen him so angry. He'd paced and walked around the camp for a long time, stopping to talk to the men, as if needing time to clear his mind. Glaring at her, he'd shaken his head, muttering words that she couldn't discern.

"You're very wet, girl. Guess you'll be suffering a while longer too, since bad girls don't get orgasms. What do bad girls get though?" He pulled his finger away from her, sticking it in his mouth, sucking loudly.

"They get…spanked."

"That they do. And naughty girls who disobey and then lie by not telling their husband, get spanked *twice*." He reached around, patting her bottom.

Her sex had been throbbing for over two hours now. He'd warned her about her spanking, making her wait until breakfast had been finished and cleaned up first, then made her stand in the corner for over half an hour. It confused her terribly. Previously, with Matt, she thought that same throbbing was caused by being scared and nervous about an impending spanking. It wasn't until

Angus had taught her about orgasms that she realized that the throbbing she felt was *sexual* — and was the anticipation, the tension that led up to her release. She loved the thrill of it, her whole body like a taut string — just a touch, and she'd go off.

"Go get your hairbrush."

Her sexual tension disappeared instantly, replaced with dread and fear. It wasn't fear that he'd hurt her — he'd never do that — but rather fear of the pain, fear of how long it may last, and fear of her reaction to it. The thought of her inevitable loss of control made her shiver. She picked up her heavy mahogany hairbrush. He'd never used it on her before, but her mother had used it on her plenty of times as a girl. She swore it hurt as bad, if not worse, than either her father's belt or the leather harness strips he kept in the barn.

She handed it to Angus, watching him rub the smooth back, slapping it hard against the palm of his hand. "This ought to teach a pretty good lesson." He set the brush down on the table next to him. "I want you to know you had nothing to do with Minnie being captured. She did this on her own. Her disobedience and strong will caused her to be kidnapped."

"But—"

He put his forefinger on her lips. "No. Not buts. You're getting punished for not telling me about what she did when I asked. And then when I specifically asked about her, you gave me no answer. Both of those are lying — by omission."

"Yes, Sir." She knew this; she'd told both of her girls the same thing.

"Lying is punishable with my belt, razor strop, or a strip of leather. You don't get many lashes, but those lashes will be laid down after a good, hard spanking. So there don't need to be many."

"Oh, Angus. I don't like the strap." She whined like a small girl, and though she hated the sound of it, but she couldn't figure any other way to get out of this — or at least convince him to go easier on her.

"I'm sure you do — but it's not meant to be pleasant. It's meant to hurt, and hurt bad enough that your ass tingles the next time you decide to lie." He drew her over his lap, settling her on his thighs. "Let's get this started."

He tapped the cold, hard wood on her bottom before pulling away and smacking it down upon the center of her backside with such force she shouted out in alarm. That first swat, no matter what the implement, always came as a shock. She clenched her muscles in preparation for the next blow.

"Nope, this isn't going to work. I don't want you to bruise, and you'll bruise clenching like that. Her pushed her over his left thigh, her buttocks now elevated and her charms no doubt on obscene display. He covered her legs with one of his own, rendering her truly unable to struggle or move, or in this position. "That's better. You won't bruise as much this way."

As much.

Then, without warning, he brought the brush down in a fast flurry of swats that had her clawing at his leg and the floor, trying to find a way to crawl away from his punishing strikes. She'd hoped she would be able to keep her cries down, since it was the middle of the day and the fellow travelers were all sitting around with nothing to do. All because of her and Minnie.

That's when it dawned on her. That was why he did it in the middle of the day — he wanted the pioneers to know that he took his job as husband and wagon master seriously. He punished her severely as an example to everyone else in the camp. He knew she wouldn't be able to contain her emotions or shouts of pain.

She knew she deserved this — and more.

Minnie, poor Minnie.

Who knew what Minnie was enduring at this very moment? She prayed that they didn't kill her or defile her.

Clara would never know how different this would have turned out if she'd told Mr. Anderson about Minnie leaving, or told Angus as soon as he returned to the camp. Yes, she deserved this punishment, and she'd take it without embarrassment — well, not *too* much, anyway — so that everyone knew she'd been soundly paddled for her offense.

Soon enough, after several rounds of the brush, her whole bottom was a raw mass of hurt. He'd made sure to give her thighs their share of strokes too, not stopping until they throbbed just as much as her poor buttocks. She sobbed pathetically, every ounce of fight drained from her as she lay limp over his lap, screeching with each new impact from the remorseless wood.

Finally, he stopped, the brush dropping to the wooden tabletop with a jarring clatter. "You think you'll be able to obey the rules now, Mrs. Warren?"

"Yes...Sir."

He lightly rubbed her bottom, soothing the scorched, aching flesh. "C'mon, time to stand up." She stood, her knees wobbling as he held her in place waiting for her legs to support her. "Put your hands on the seat of the chair, legs shoulder width apart."

"Oh, no! Angus, I just can't!" She clasped her hands to her bottom, shaking her head at him. She felt desperate, like she might run and actually looked toward the flap of the tent.

"Girl, don't even think about it. You can't handle the paddling you just received." He raised both his eyebrows at her, in shock. "You want more? Is that what you really want?"

"N-no. I don't. But, please don't use your belt, Angus." Her lip quivered. "*Please.*" She hated that she'd resorted to begging, but she couldn't imagine how she'd handle more.

He paused, watching her closely. Was he actually going to relent?

"I'm not backing down. Bad girls who lie receive the

belt. Period. It's just the way it is. I know you don't think you can handle more, but you will." He took his belt off, folding it in his hand, palming the buckle. "I won't be doing you any favors if you think some tears and begging will stay my hand. You need to know that once I give my word, I won't back down."

She stared at the large hand holding the thick, brown belt. Her legs started to shake again.

"Bend over, girl. I won't say it again."

She pivoted, facing the black spindle-back chair, placing her hands flat on the seat.

He tapped his booted foot on the inside of her ankle. "Open your legs."

Her voice broke into a sob as she widened her stance, knowing the position revealed everything. Her fear of her punishment and the pain in her bottom had overwhelmed her arousal though.

"They'll be fast and hard. You're only getting a dozen. You won't lie to me again, girlie."

He kept a hand on her lower back and started thrashing her buttocks. On top of the freshly paddled skin, the leather stung like a thousand bee stings. She squeezed the edge of the chair seat with her hands, but when it became too much, her knees started to bend so deeply she thought she might fall to the floor.

Angus wrapped an arm around her waist, tucking her to his hip. "Only four more, girl." He gave them fast, dropping the belt to the floor when he'd finished, enveloping her in his warm embrace. He held her, both of them swaying together until her breathing returned to normal, her cries reduced to sniffling.

"Please promise me that you won't *ever* make me do that again. Now, it's time to stand in the corner and think about how you'll do things differently from now on." He walked her over to a sewn seam of the tent. "Except, I'm doing this different too. Bend at the waist and stand still."

Clara peeked over her shoulder watching as he reached

over to the table, picking up a white candle, quickly turning her face to the wall of the tent when he came back to her. He poured the wax onto her lower back just above her right cheek, the warmth spreading to her spine, relaxing her.

"I'm pooling the wax into a small area so I can place the candle into the thickened wax. This candle will drip down your spanked cheek. It won't burn your quim or your anus, but it will cover the cheek and thigh, sealing in the heat already present. It won't be pleasant, but it shouldn't be overly painful either. If it becomes painful, you let me know, sweetie. Okay?"

"Yes, Sir. It just burns a little."

He pulled his chair right up behind her. "I'll be right here watching and ready to catch the candle should it come lose. It'll burn a little more than last night, but it'll keep that red flesh hot so you can think about what caused your punishment today."

"Yes, Sir."

The wax slowly slid down her spanked bottom, and he'd been right about one thing: it stung as it made the trek down to her thigh. His fingers wandered over her flesh, sliding into her sex. He anchored another candle above her left cheek while he delved deep into the secret places of her body. He blew lightly on the cooling wax and flicked her clit, drawing her right to the edge of the cliff. Then he pulled away, slapping her hip. He would stoke the fires only to dampen them again. Reaching through her legs, his hand grasped one of her breasts, twisting the nipple, pinching and tugging until she moaned, her hips jerking in response. Her reaction made the wax dribble close to her little back hole.

"Oh, Angus. It's so close to my..." She didn't want to even say it out loud to him.

"Oh, yes, I see it, girl. It's not getting that close, but I bet it burns on that sensitive skin. That skin is so tender. Imagine if I spanked that area too."

Spank her ...back there? Do people do that?

"W-would you...you can't. Would you really do that to me?"

"Oh, most definitely. If I thought you deserved it, or you did something that warranted such a painful punishment, I wouldn't hesitate. Does that scare you? Or does the thought of having your little pink rosebud spanked turn you on, girl?" He pressed his thumb against the little pucker, but didn't push it through the tight muscles there. Not yet, anyway. She clenched and unclenched, feeling the work-roughened pad of his thumb stroke back and forth over her tender entrance.

"Jesus, that's hot. I felt your little asshole wink under my thumb." He pressed into her, and she reflexively tried to stand up, forgetting the candle for a moment.

"Don't!" Angus shouted, and she immediately moved back into position, her slight movement thankfully not enough to upset the lit candle.

"You'll stay still and let me finger your little ass. I wish you could see this the way I'm seeing it. Your beautiful, rosy pink ass with visible hair brush marks on your hips, bent over with white wax dripping down your freshly spanked backside. It's just fucking sexy, Clara."

His finger lightly traced the drip marks on her bottom. "And now my right hand is covering your other cheek, my thumb in your little hole, the scent of your arousal filling my nostrils while your sweet honey is coating that fine blonde hair on your cute little cunt." He exhaled loudly, his breath blowing lightly over her sex, his thumb pumping slowly into her dark hole.

"Oh, God, Angus! I'm going to come. Is that...please?" She knew her voice sounded strangled, her teeth gritted so hard, her molars hurt. If he said no, she'd just have to be punished — because she had hit the point of no return.

"Good girl. Yes, you may come." He pulled out of her ass only to jam a finger into her fast and hard, pumping quickly, another finger sliding into her pussy, flicking her clit. It took every ounce of her strength, but she stayed bent over, not moving from her position as her sex convulsed, contracting hard with her orgasm. She clamped a fist between her teeth, trying to stifle the sound of her growling moan, her cum releasing, the warm fluid gushing from her sex, wetness dripping from her labia.

Still bent over, Clara panted, trying to catch her breath, the sudden smell of sulfur strong in the tent as he extinguished the candle. "Stay bent over. I gotta scrape the wax off your bottom. It's going to hurt some since you have a naughty spanked backside."

The knife blade scraped along her flesh, unpeeling the wax as it went along, causing her to wiggle and whine under the pain, but overall, she kept quiet and patiently held her position. It was the least she could do. It was undoubtedly less than what poor Minnie was enduring at that moment.

The process had been time consuming and by the time Angus finished getting the last bit of wax off of her, she'd had to wipe away a few tears. Relief didn't begin to describe how she felt, now that it was over.

"Come here, girl." She pivoted toward him, his warm smile, and outstretched arms beckoning her forth. She couldn't help but dash toward him, rushing into the safety of those large, muscular arms, letting herself be enveloped by him. His chest hair tickled her nose as she inhaled, smelling soap, leather, horses — and Angus. She'd never tire of him, that smell alone awakening her sexually. She pressed her hips against him, the hard ridge of his cock pressing into her belly.

"Let's find a way to save your ass from any more friction, and give me what I want too. I need a rider today. Wanna go for a ride, girl?" He sat in the wooden chair, his penis jutting up, jerking with his arousal.

"I think I might like that, Mr. Warren." She straddled him, his large hands on each hip hoisting her up, then guiding her down upon him. She bit her lip at the delicious feel of the deep penetration, his cock wide and long, the ridges stroking and rubbing all the right places inside, causing her head to roll back in ecstasy, her eyes closing. She swiveled her hips, sliding slowly up and down his length, leaning forward so her clit would be caressed by the silky smooth skin of his turgid member. She clenched her inner muscles around him on the way up, listening to him moan as he gripped her hips, his fingers digging into the plump flesh of her ass.

He tugged her closer to him, pounding into her. She rose up, pressing her toes into the ground below her. "Wait. Do I get to be in control when I'm sitting like this?"

"What?" He looked confused, eyebrows furrowed.

"Do I get to control what happens and when it happens, when I'm on top of you, like you do when you're on top of me?" She ran her hands lightly over his shoulders. She loved the feel of those hard muscles under her fingers.

"I guess. I don't like to give up much control, so I may change my mind without much warning.

But you can try to be in control for a while." He shrugged and then his lips curled in a lopsided grin. "Might be fun to see what you do with a little control in bed."

"I like being in charge sometimes too, you know."

"Can't say I'm really shocked by that, Mrs. Warren. Sorry if you were expecting an argument."

She smiled at him. He had no idea how much fun she'd have with this. "Hands on the chair or behind your head," she barked out at him, making sure she used his words against him.

He narrowed his gaze at her, slowly putting his hands behind his head. His cock twitched inside her, and she clenched around it, listening to his rumble from deep in his chest.

She twirled her hips, rising slowly, painfully so judging by the way he grit his teeth. She clenched tightly on the

glide up, releasing her grip on him on the slide down —
which she also made excruciatingly slow. While her hips
made the slow, torturous journey, she scraped her
thumbnails lightly over his nipples, nibbling along his neck
and collarbone. She sat back, sliding and swiveling,
watching his face tighten, his teeth clench. She bit his lips,
slipping her tongue into his mouth, teasing him, sliding her
tongue along the roof of his mouth. She pulled away with
a lazy smile, waggling her eyebrows at him.

"Damn it, woman. I ain't going to last like this
forever."

"Oh you'll last, don't you worry." He jerked his hips,
trying to pound into her. She leaned back, her hands upon
his thighs, stilling her hips from any movement at all,
perfectly motionless — and not allowing him to move
either. She clenched his cock as hard as she could, but still
didn't move, watching his eyes close with a groan.

"Done. I'm in charge!" he snarled, pulling her hands
off his thighs and grabbing her hips once more, his fingers
digging into her spanked flesh. He proceeded to bounce
her off his cock, pounding within her, the head rubbing
against the mouth of her womb on each deep thrust. This
time it was Angus who lost control, and he moaned and
shouted with his release, sending her over the cliff with her
own. He continued to pound into her, her orgasm milking
every last drop of his come.

They clung to each other, quietly recovering until he
swatted her bottom, making her cry out.

"Think you're pretty funny with what you did there,"
he said. "You proud of yourself?"

She couldn't hide her smile. "Yes, as a matter of fact, I
am. It felt good to watch you come apart under my
control. Is that how you feel?"

"I reckon I do feel that way. I don't relinquish my
control often…but I may like giving it up to you." She sat
up straight with excitement. "Don't get too damn excited.
It won't be all the time, but I kinda liked watching this side

of Mrs. Warren."

CHAPTER SEVENTEEN

Minnie looked around at the men now that they were all standing at the counter at the local inn in Independence. They were a seedy crew and she hoped that it raised the innkeeper's eyebrows a little to see a clean and well-dressed woman with three men who looked exactly like the outlaws they were. She'd just left this place a couple days ago, and hoped that maybe someone would remember her or place her as someone who'd been on the Widow Wagon.

The innkeeper came to the counter, and, just as she hoped, he looked her up and down, slipping a furtive glance at the men before addressing them directly. "How are you men doing today?"

"We need two rooms." Red spoke up for them all.

"No. We need three rooms." Kane glared at Red. "I ain't sleeping with you again. You snore too much." Red's teeth were such a mess that Minnie had a hard time even looking at him. He turned and spit into a spittoon, wiping his mouth with the back of his hand.

He noticed her watching him. "What the fuck are you lookin' at?"

She jumped at the harshness of his voice, backing up a

step toward Silas, dropping her gaze to the floor. Once again, Silas seemed like the safest captor, and at least she knew he'd keep her safer than Red would.

"Shut yer trap, Red." Silas pulled her behind him, stepping up to the counter. "We — the lady and I — need our own room, Sir." He cocked a thumb toward his companions. "Those two will have their own room."

"Is that okay with you, little lady?" The innkeeper leaned toward her. "Do you know this man in that kind of manner?"

She looked to over at Silas, and one eyebrow shot up as he dipped his chin. The last thing she wanted was to be in a room with a man she didn't know, but when given the choice between Silas, Red, of Kane, she'd pick Silas any day.

"Yes, Sir, I'm fine with that," she said, looking the innkeeper in the eye. "Thank you for asking."

He narrowed his gaze at her, pen in hand with the guestbook open. "As owner of this Inn, it's my job to ensure the safety — moral or otherwise — of my guests. If there's an issue, you let me know."

"Just what are you saying here? You got a problem with us and our situation here?" Red pulled his gun out of his gun belt and stood with it staring down at the man. "Cuz if you do, you need to talk to us men, not some silly snot-nosed woman."

The innkeeper put both hands up, though his gaze didn't falter one bit. "Son, I suggest you put that gun away. I don't have a problem with any of you, and if you want a room here, pulling a gun on me ain't going to make it happen any faster. Trust me. I'm just checking with the woman here, not meaning to cause any trouble."

Silas pushed Red's gun down. "Put that goddamn thing away, Red. Christ, are you that tired and ornery?" He leaned on the counter, smiling at the man. "He hasn't had any sleep in a couple days and is just cantankerous."

Sighing, the innkeeper signed them all into the

guestbook and handed the keys for the rooms to Silas.

They trudged up the stairs, the steps wooden and dusty. Minnie couldn't help but wonder when someone had last cleaned. A long runner, burgundy with a white swirled pattern, led down a hallway, dark wooden doors to the left and right. Silas handed the men their keys when they got to the top of the stairs, then looked for the room he and Minnie would occupy.

"Wait a dang minute!" Kane had his hands on his hips, glaring at both Minnie and Silas. "Are you getting to fuck her tonight? I thought I'd get a chance at her."

Red hit him in the shoulder. "Silas already has a shine to her, so I said he could he could have her. I had Annie. The next bitch we pick up will be yours. I promise. Let Silas have her. She's too uppity for you anyway. Look at her."

Both Red and Kane sized her up, their gazes traveling up from her toes to the top of her head and back again. She opened her mouth to tell the dirty, filthy varmints off, but Silas dug his nails into the inside of her wrist hard enough that she swallowed her words — and her outrage.

"Yeah, she's probably as cold as a fish in bed." Red elbowed Kane, his laughter loud and harsh. "Let Silas try to warm that up."

"Put your shit in your room," Red said. "Let's go to the saloon and find us a woman who knows how to make a man happy."

* * *

After sitting in a chair, she silently watched Silas gracefully move around, putting the contents of his bag into the dresser, the man taking a minute to wash his face, then comb his hair. They only had one bed, and two chairs seated around a small table. She looked around, finding no cot or anything else that could even be considered as an alternate place to sleep. The bed had a clean, handmade quilt on top, with blue and red patterned hearts. The curtains were dark blue velvet; when closed, the guests would be able to sleep undisturbed by the daylight outside the window. There was a privacy screen in one corner, a pitcher and washbasin on a stand with an attached mirror.

But there was only one bed.

How would they sleep tonight? He'd said he'd 'fuck her' and the others had said he'd taken a 'shine' to her.

Yes, she'd decided she was marrying a man she'd never seen before in Idaho, and she'd been married before — but that certainly didn't mean she would cotton to being violated. Things like that ruined women for life. She looked him over as he moved about the room. He wasn't as vile as Red and Kane. He definitely cleaned up better. His teeth were clean, and unlike his partners, he still had all of them. His clothes, although dirty from the trail, didn't reek of body odor. He kept his long hair tied at the base of his neck, and it looked clean. When he washed his face, he'd untied the leather strip from the dark locks, combing it out. Long, brown waves, blessed with a little curl, hung down to his shoulders. His beard wasn't scraggily like Red's, but instead had been neatly trimmed. He didn't seem to chew either, as his facial hair wasn't filthy with the disgusting juice. Yet another way he differed from his companions.

But no matter how he looked or how he had acted, he'd kidnapped her. She needed to make her escape before nightfall, or she'd be forced to sleep with him, letting him fuck her like a dirty whore in the saloon. She'd never find a husband again if it ever got out that she'd been defiled in Wyoming.

The other two were downstairs right now, no doubt trying to find a saloon gal to sleep with. Silas didn't seem like them in that regard either. She wondered how he'd come to know them. Had he killed many men? Or violated women? Did he take a woman's virginity against her will? He was larger than most men, and she had no doubt that he'd be able to subdue a woman easily, holding her to a bed against her will. But was he capable of such callousness? Even if he violated her, would he still hold her afterward? Would he wipe away her tears, or would he just throw on his clothes and leave her to deal with the physical and emotional pain left in his wake?

"You okay, sweetheart?" He sat down in the other chair at the table next to her, and he didn't seem to be making fun of her either. He appeared genuinely concerned that she might not be okay.

How silly is that?

He'd kidnapped her, beaten her bottom raw with his belt, and was talking openly about fucking her, and yet he wanted to know if she was okay?

"No. I'm scared and...I guess I'm hungry too."

"I bet you are scared. I don't blame you there. Thank you for being honest. I'm sure that wasn't easy to admit. And after the spanking I gave you, you must be sore and frightened of me. Am I right?"

She hesitated. She really didn't want to talk about the fact that her bottom was still throbbing, and that it indeed did make her more afraid of him. The last thing she wanted to do was upset him and have that hand or belt applied to her backside yet again.

"Yes, Sir."

He nodded, looking down at the table for a moment. "A little fear isn't a bad thing. I need you to mind me and do as I say. I want to keep you safe from Red...well, and Kane too. But I don't want you *too* afraid of me though.

You feel free to come to me with anything they may say or do that scares you. You hear?"

"Yes, Sir. I will." She swallowed against the tightness in her throat. *Everything* Red did or said scared her. She'd probably be talking to Silas every five minutes, truth be told.

"I'm hungry too," Silas said. "There's a great little place to eat here that makes home-cooked meals. Let's go get some dinner before we go to bed. Morning will be here early."

He stood up abruptly, holding his hand out to her. "I need to stop at the telegraph office first. It will just be a moment to send a message, then we'll go straight to Ma's Place."

"Your *mother* lives here?"

He chuckled. "Nah, that's what Kate's restaurant is called — Ma's Place — and she owns it. Once you have some of her food you'll see why people call it that."

* * *

They came back to the room, and as promised, the food had been just like her Ma had cooked. It made her miss her family back in North Carolina. When she'd married Beau, she never thought she'd be a widow in less than a year. The damned war. How many of her friends lost brothers and fathers to The Cause?

At the time, all she cared about was marrying a soldier, someone handsome in a uniform at their wedding. She loved him — as much as anyone at seventeen can love a man. And even now, at almost nineteen, she felt so much older than she'd been then. As a small child, she played house with her brothers and sisters. Marrying Beau had that same feeling of almost...unreality. She remembered feeling that at any minute her mother would call her for dinner and it'd be over. Instead, it had been the knock on the door with a young sober-faced soldier ending her dream.

Her days of playing house had ended abruptly indeed.

So, when the ad in the newspaper said there was a Widow Wagon heading west, she'd packed her trunk and they'd given her a name of man in Idaho — Mr. Thomas Ferris. The man who'd become her new husband, building a life with her in a new home out West.

And that dream too ended as she'd been thrown recklessly over a horse at the point of a gun. More than likely, she'd be defiled tonight by Silas and her reputation would be in tatters. She'd be known for the rest of her life as poor Widow Johnson. People would whisper behind their hands or fans about what happened years ago to Poor Widow Johnson.

"What was that sigh for?" Silas patiently stood, waiting for an answer.

Oh, shit! She didn't realize that she'd done that out loud.

"Nothing. Just tired, I guess."

He stared for a moment, as if he knew she wasn't telling the truth. Then he said, "Yeah, I'm tired too." He tipped his head toward the privacy screen. "Why don't you go over there and get out of that dress. At least you can sleep in your chemise. Might be a little more comfortable."

"I couldn't...why, it wouldn't be—"

"I'm not taking no as an answer. Go change." His tone made her belly flip and her ass tingle. It had just stopped throbbing, and she didn't want to give him the opportunity to reawaken the ache in her bottom. She walked briskly behind the privacy screen, starting to undo the ties at the back of her skirt, only to jump at the timbre of his deep voice behind her. "Let me undo these buttons for you or you'll never get this off."

He deftly undid the buttons on her dress, then unlaced the ties on her corset, leaving her to take them off privately. Pushing them off her shoulders, she let them fall to the floor. She picked them up and neatly folded them over the top of the screen. Before she could come out from behind the screen, there was a loud knock on their door. She stayed where she was, hidden from view.

Silas' booted feet clomped on the floorboards as he walked to the door, opening it. "What do you want?"

"We wanna see if Minnie is naked in bed. Did you fuck her yet, Silas?"

Red.

Of course, it was Red with his crude and crass remarks.

"We wanted to see if you'd let us watch. We'll just sit over there and watch you two. Won't say a word!" Kane sounded drunk, the both of them even more obnoxious than usual.

"No, you can't watch!" Silas barked. "What in the name of hell do you think this is? Get the fuck out of here before I knock you both out." There was a bit of shuffling, and she realized he was pushing them back out to the hallway.

"I'm tellin' ya, Silas, if we don't hear some noise coming from this room — something that says you're taking her — we're coming back to take her to our room.

If we can't see it, we damn well better hear it!"

Oh, God! They want to hear her screaming?

She stood with her hand to her chest, hoping if she pressed hard enough that she'd be able to make her heart stop beating so hard. Maybe she should try to escape now? Where would she go though? The Sheriff. She'd go to the Sheriff's office, tell him she'd been kidnapped, and he'd bring her back to the Widow Wagon. She'd have to plan her escape though — she didn't want to get caught. Silas wasn't a man to trifle with.

"Don't you worry about seeing or hearing anything. What I do isn't any of your fucking business!" Silas slammed the door, and stood silently, breathing so hard she could hear it across the room.

"I know you're ready, so come out here." He'd said it so gruffly, she wanted to curl up in a corner instead. But she took a deep breath and moved around the screen to find him standing in the middle of the floor, hands on his hips, the large belt buckle on his belt gleaming, catching the light from the nearby oil lantern on the night stand.

Although the room was stifling hot — and in spite of the breeze blowing the lacy sheers on the windows — she crossed her arms over her chest, hiding herself from his gaze.

"I have sisters, you don't have to worry about your body. I've seen girls...and women in their chemise before." He pointed to a chair. "Sit."

She didn't know how to answer that, so she sat in silence. He walked over to a small table, picking up a glass decanter filled with amber liquid and pouring a thumb of that liquor into one of the sparkling crystal glasses. He set the glass down in front of her. "Drink it."

"I don't like whiskey or liquor." She pushed the glass away with the tips of her fingers.

"I didn't ask if you liked it, I said to drink it. It'll calm your nerves and make this easier."

This.

He was now referring to her ruination as *this*. Would she call it that for the rest of her life too? Probably. She'd say to friends, "I had promise, I had a future and then *this* happened." Or "People have no idea what it feels like to have something like *this* happen. Things like *this* change you for life."

If it would calm her nerves and make it easier, she'd do it. She picked up the glass, took a deep breath, and drank it all down, barely letting the liquid touch her tongue. She slammed the glass onto the table...and jumped up, her throat feeling as if she'd swallowed fire. Even breathing seemed suddenly difficult, and she flailed her arms, beginning to panic.

"Jesus H. Christ, girl, what did you do? You aren't supposed to swallow it all at once." He leapt over to her, slapping her on the back so hard that she forgot she couldn't breathe and drew in a great gasping breath.

Silas filled a glass with water, handing it to her. "Drink this." Then he added hastily as she grabbed desperately for it. "No! Just sip it!"

She narrowed her gaze at him. He didn't need to treat her like she was a feeble-minded woman. Sipping the water at least somewhat soothed the liquid fire in her throat.

"Thank you, Silas, even though you could've warned me of the effects of swallowing it too fast." She pushed the tumbler at him, taking a seat in the chair.

He walked to the liquor cabinet, setting the glass on top. "I didn't think you'd be that green about alcohol. And don't think I missed that glare either. Watch your attitude, missy."

It didn't take long for her to feel a little woozy, her lips beginning to go slightly numb. She thought she might like having a little more, despite the burn. If a little felt good, more would feel even better, right?

She pointed to her glass on the cabinet. "I think I'd like another glass of that whiskey, Silas."

He leaned back in his chair, studying her face for a

151

moment before taking his booted foot off of his knee, rising gracefully without a word. His long fingers, tan with clean, neatly filed nail beds, seemed out of place for an outlaw. The backs of his hands were thin, the bones defined and easily seen with large veins prominently displayed. She knew from 'hands on experience' that those thin, wide hands packed a wallop; she still couldn't sit comfortably on the wooden chairs.

He held the amber liquid in front of her. "Do you think you can handle this, girl? Or should I feed it to you like you're a child?"

"There's no need to be condescending, Silas. I'm getting a little tired of you treating me like I'm some imbecile. I'm a cultured, intelligent woman. But on second thought, maybe that's your problem. You don't know what to do with a woman like me. Hmph." She turned in her chair, lifting her chin and closing her eyes to sip the whiskey — gently and slowly this time.

After she put the glass down, he still stood in front of her, pulling her to her feet, cupping her chin in his one hand while the other squeezed her still sore spanked bottom, squeezing it and making her gasp.

"Oh, don't doubt for a second think that I don't know what to do with you, girlie. I believe this little ass, if I'm guessing correctly, is still throbbing from the attention I gave it. And if you keep it up, I'll dust it a little more before you get sent to bed to cry yourself to sleep."

He stood so close that the hard bulge in his pants pressed against her soft belly. She tried to pull away, only to have him pull her in tighter. "Do you think you might want to sit on your little tail and drink quietly now? Or should I impress upon you that I do *indeed* know how to handle a cultured, intelligent, sassy-mouthed woman in need of a lesson?"

"Uhm..." She felt her face flush. "I think I'd like to sit down now, Sir."

"I like hearing you call me 'Sir.' By all means, Miss

Minnie, sit down and behave."

She watched him walk back to his chair. The black pants and long sleeve shirt he wore only made him look more dangerous. He'd changed to that outfit before they left for dinner and she had to admit he cleaned up nicely. Funny how Red and Kane stayed in their clothes and didn't appear to have cleaned up at all. She had so many questions about Silas, but as her captor, she found herself wondering why she even cared about those little details.

He moved like a lion, smooth, slow, graceful. He slid into his chair, crossing his right ankle onto his left knee. With his elbow on the table, he cupped his face with his thumb and forefinger, like men do when they are thinking or regarding someone — or something — intently.

"So, tell me, Minnie, how did you end up in this situation? Getting kidnapped. Because I'm assuming that your wagon master had rules to keep his women safe on this passage west." His booted foot jiggled on his knee. He had huge feet. The boots were well-kept, as with everything else about him. He seemed to care for the details — keeping his beard trimmed, brushing his teeth, keeping his boots oiled. Perhaps there was even more he cared about.

Minnie cleared her throat. "Angus did have rules." She stopped there, not sure she liked where this discussion was heading.

He quirked an eyebrow at her. "Such as?"

"Well, we were supposed to tell him that we needed to attend to our lady business. And then we would have to go with a partner, while he stood at a safe distance with his gun. We weren't supposed to be alone — *ever.*"

"Mmm. As I suspected. " He dropped his leg, leaning forward, lacing his fingers between his knees. "So tell me, girl. Did you chafe under those rules?"

"I did. I didn't like them. Women should have their privacy. One day we — the women on the Widow Wagon — got into a bit of a...fight. And I ran off by myself to sit in an alley alone in Independence — actually not far from where we are now. So, yes, Angus knew I didn't like the rules." She looked down at her hands.

He was silent for a long moment, and she lifted her head, watching him.

"So what happened when he finally found you in the alley?"

"Do I have to answer all these questions?" She furrowed her eyebrows. Exactly who the hell did he think he was asking all these damn questions? If he was going to defile her, he needed to just get it over with. They weren't courtin' or anything.

"Yes. I want answers. And keep your attitude in check. I won't say it again."

"He dragged me back to the wagon and in front of all the women who'd traveled with me, and all the other pioneers stationed there with us, he spanked my bare bottom with a large handmade paddle he carries with him." The blush flooded up her neck, rising up her face, engulfing her in the heat of embarrassment. She refused to look at him. He probably took great enjoyment in her retelling the story.

"I think I like Angus already. I'm going to be glad to make his acquaintance someday." He reached across the table, lifting her chin with his long forefinger. "You deserved every bit of that, and obviously more because you *still* disobeyed and went off by yourself."

"I wanted to relieve myself in peace. I didn't want to be watched by some damn woman."

He leaned forward. "That may be so, but instead you're now in my room, sitting in your chemise with those peach nipples poking through your see-through chemise. And soon you'll be naked under my body, while I penetrate your hot, moist sex with my hard-as-steel cock. And if you're a good girl, I'll make you scream in ecstasy, begging me to take you again."

She swallowed so loud, she had no doubt he heard it.

As vulgar as those words were, her sex pulsed, and she wondered if he really could make her scream. What would it feel like to have his muscled frame on top of her, bringing her to heights that Beau never seemed able to bring her to? Her hand brought her to higher heights than her husband did most days. It had been a long time since she'd been pounded with a hard penis, and her clit seemed to relish the thought of Silas doing exactly as he promised. Could he actually make her beg for more? She imagined her hands clawing that muscled back, squeezing the bunched muscles of his taut ass as he pistoned his cock into her.

Dear Lord, I've lost my fucking mind! He's a renegade, an outlaw, and a kidnapper. I'm a renegade's captive.

"You like the sound of begging me, girl?" He winked at her with that dimple showing in his cheek.

"I have no idea what you're talking about." She turned in her chair, rubbing her bottom in the process and gasping.

"That little tail is still sore, isn't it? Should keep you obedient. If not, I know the cure."

She didn't even acknowledge he'd spoken, keeping her head turned. At that moment, merely looking at him was too much. She stared out the window, listening to the sounds of the town outside. Raucous music from the nearby saloon. The whistling of a gentleman walking under the window. Children laughing and playing where the wagons were camped for the night.

She could run. If she got to the door, all she had to do was open it and dash down the stairs. She couldn't stand the thought of all those men in the saloon seeing her in her chemise, but even that would be better than what Silas had in store for her. And, God forbid, far preferable to anything Red or Kane intended to do to her.

His eyes closed. Had he fallen asleep? She rustled in her chair to see if he startled awake. He didn't. It was time. This was her chance.

She leapt up, running for the door.

CHAPTER EIGHTEEN

W*hen in the name of hell did I fall asleep?*

He woke just as Minnie flew through the door to the room, running toward the stairs. The chemise clung to her round ass, every wobble and shake visible through the sheer fabric. He leapt to his feet.

"Damn it! Minnie get your ass back here! Now!"

She screeched at the sound of his voice but quickened her pace, flying down the stairs with him hot on her trail. Behind him, he heard Red shouting, "You can't keep track of one little slip of a woman?"

"Son of bitch! Leave this alone, Red. I'll handle her." The last thing he needed was Red deciding he'd take her. He'd fight the man — and win. He wouldn't watch him assault another woman. The man was just evil to his core. What Red did to grown men frightened him. After witnessing what Red had done to women in the past, Silas vowed he'd never let Minnie fall into the foul man's clutches.

She had made it down the stairs and just past the piano player when Silas caught up to her, grabbing her around the waist and tossing her over his shoulder.

"Let me go!" She screamed, pounding on his back with

her small fists. "He's going to hurt me! I've been kidnapped!"

He laughed, looking at the men as he started back up the staircase. "She likes playing that I'm a kidnapper. Says if she's a 'victim' the sex is easier. Thank you all for obliging us in our little games!" He slapped her ass hard, the sound of the smack echoing through the saloon amidst cheers and clapping. "Come, naughty wench, time for me to plunder what belongs to me!"

He marched up the steps, his heart beating in his throat, wondering if anyone would question him and take her away. Fortunately, no one followed. He made it to the top of the stairs, still hearing the catcalls and whistles from the onlookers.

Now, he had to deal with Red and Kane who stood blocking entrance to their room.

"Jesus, Silas if you can't handle her, I'll take her." Kane elbowed Red as he said it. "I haven't had a woman yet, and she wouldn't have gotten away with *me* on top of her."

"No, shit! I don't believe I've ever had one get away either." Red eyed Minnie's ass, the thin chemise leaving nothing to the imagination. "Are ya that green that you don't know how to handle her?"

"She's mine. Y'all stay away. I've got some disciplining to do and then I'm taking her as mine. Now leave us be to carry on." He pushed past them, giving each man a glare. He'd fight both of them — kill them, if he had to. No one was taking her away.

He opened the door to the room, closing it behind them and throwing the bolt before he lowered her on the floor. She stood with that brown hair curling around her face, making her look even younger than he suspected she was. She didn't look a day over twenty, but standing in her chemise with her hair down, an adorable curl laying across her forehead, she looked like a teenager to him. At thirty-one, he felt so much older than she was, that age difference amplifying the protectiveness he felt toward young women. How could she run into a saloon full of drunk men looking for some action, the silly girl wearing nothing but her chemise?

"What in tarnation were you thinking, girl? Those men down there would have leapt on you, taking you before I could wake to your screams. I've never seen anyone do something so dangerous." He paced, raking his hands through his hair. He didn't even want to think of what could've happened if he'd fallen into a deep sleep. "Apparently, your ass isn't sore any longer. But I think I'll remedy that right now. Take everything off. You won't be needing clothes for either activity I've got planned for you."

She wrung her hands, her deep blue eyes filling with tears. "I had to run. I had to try to protect myself. I need to be able to tell people that I tried, that I ran. Even if I didn't succeed, I can tell people I did my best."

"And I need to be able to say the same thing. I told you that if you listened, I'd protect you." He took off his gun belt putting it up high on an armoire.

"But who's going to protect me from you?"

He had to give her credit. She had more gumption than a dozen women put together. He couldn't answer that question though — not now.

First things, first.

"Clothes off," he said, clenching his jaw.

Her small hands shook as she pulled the chemise over her head, leaving her standing in her full glory. The curls at the apex of her pale, white thighs caught his attention first. He swore his mouth started to water. She had an hourglass figure that had been buried among the layers of cloth meant to bury a woman's figure. Her breasts weren't overly large, but definitely would be more than a handful. Although the evening was warm, her nipples were erect and hard and all he wanted to do was let those little nubs rub on the palms of his hands.

He unbuttoned his shirt, watching her eyes widen as he

slipped it off his shoulders.

"Why…are you taking your shirt off?"

"It's hot in here, and I plan on working up a sweat spanking your naughty ass."

"Oh, no!" She started to cry quietly, covering her face with her hands. He had no doubt in his mind that her bottom had to be sore, and that this wouldn't be easy — for either of them. But she'd left him no choice.

"Oh, yes. Come here, sweetheart." He pulled his chair away from the table, taking a seat, crooking his finger for her to come to him.

If she had a fifty-pound weight chained to her leg, she couldn't have walked slower. "There ain't nothing to discuss. Let's just get this out of the way."

He tugged on her hand, laying her over his lap, situating her so her bottom was just right. He ran his hand over her still pink buttocks, her skin still displaying the darker pink stripes left by his belt. Some areas were pale purple and she flinched when he pressed on them. He'd do his best to avoid them, but it wouldn't be easy.

He patted her soft, plump flesh a couple times in warning and then landed crisp, hard slaps, leaving red handprints in his wake until he'd turned the whole of her bottom into a dark shade of pink. He focused some of his swats on her thighs, and she screeched, rocking her hips, trying to avoid his hand. He'd teach her soon that he'd never permit such behavior from a woman being spanked.

The screeches soon became loud wails, and he finally stopped, rubbing her bottom. "Do you know what could have happened if I didn't wake up? Those men would have taken you. Or Red or Kane would have grabbed you, *both* of them taking you. Where did you think you were going, dressed like that? Did you think it through at all?"

She sputtered and coughed through her sobs. "I wanted to g-go to the Sheriff. I didn't th-think about Red or K-Kane. I just had to run."

He had to admit, running to the sheriff was a good

plan. And Buck would have kept her safe too. But as Silas had told her, that would only be the case if she'd escaped Red, Kane and all the other men.

He stood her up, keeping his hands at her waist to steady her. The spicy scent from her sex drifted to his nostrils and his cock hardened. He fought the urge to stroke her little pussy. She struggled, looking embarrassed, trying to hide her breasts and sex from him, rubbing her sore hind end.

"Get my hairbrush."

"Nooooo!" Her hands covered her bottom, and she started to whine, bouncing on her feet until she realized that her breasts were jiggling in his face.

"Yes." He pointed to where the brush laid. "Get it. *Now.*"

She scurried to the washstand, walking back quickly with the brush in her outstretched hand. He stood up from his chair, bending her over and tucking her against his hip. "There won't be many with this punishment, but I'm focusing most of them on your sit spot and thighs. Your bottom just can't handle much more."

The brush was heavy in his hand and he made sure the first wallop with it left an impression. He overlapped the swats, alternating blows to both legs. Then he laid down a flurry of smacks from the underside of her buttocks to the tops of each thigh, repeating it several times until her whimpers become one continuous wail. She danced on her toes, trying to tuck her bottom in to avoid the brutal wood.

He threw the brush onto the table with a loud clatter, rubbing her bottom and thighs. "Do you think you might listen to me now and do as you're told?"

"Yes, Sir!"

He wiped her face with his handkerchief. "Damn, you scared the shit out of me. I don't want to wake up like that *ever* again."

She stared at him, nodding her head. She'd be lying on

her belly over the horse tomorrow. Sitting in a saddle would not be an option.

He backed away from her, undoing his belt.

"Oh, no!"

"No, no, that's not happening. You're done. It's time to get on with the second part of your night." He slid his pants down his legs, dropping his drawers. Minnie stared at him shamelessly, then her face paled, and she shook her head, backing away from him, panic in her eyes.

He grabbed her, laying her on the bed, holding her struggling hands over her head as he laid on top of her slight frame. When she opened her mouth to scream, he covered it with his hand, reducing her wail to little more than a muffled squawk. He whispered into her ear, "Listen. Minnie, listen to me! Now! Stop!"

She stilled. He'd given her enough ass whoopin's today that she knew to listen to his commands. No doubt fear was the foremost emotion warring within her.

"You need to listen to me." He locked his gaze with hers. "Are you listening?"

She nodded vigorously. Those large blue doe-eyes tore his heart out. He hoped he wasn't crushing her, but she seemed to be breathing fine. Such a petite woman.

"I'm a U.S. Marshal. I'm not a renegade or an outlaw." He paused to let the words sink in. She blinked several times — a good sign. He pulled his hand off her mouth slowly, keeping it close just in case she thought to cry out again.

"You're a...marshal?" Her voice had dropped to little more than a whisper.

"Yes. I'm not going to defile you. I'm doing this so if Red or Kane sneak a peek through a window or door, they will think it's happening." He paused a moment, watching her closely. "I will *not* ruin you. Do you hear?"

She nodded again.

"My job is to keep you safe. I've contacted the U.S. Marshal's office in Wyoming and the Sheriff at Devil's

Gate. The posse and Marshals should be here tomorrow before the sun is up to arrest them — and return you safely to the Widow Wagon."

She started to quietly cry, tears running down the sides of her face into her hair. He wiped them with the pad of his thumbs. "Don't cry. It'll be okay. I'm sorry I scared you so bad, but I know these men. They're evil and conniving. I had to make sure it looked like I took you if they found a way to watch. If they're watching now, they'll think I took you and it's over. You're safe, Minnie. Just make sure you listen to me and do everything I say until they're arrested."

"I will. I promise." She threw her arms around his neck, crying in relief. He needed to get off of her though. His cock didn't care about the circumstances, it just knew that there was a warm, soft woman beneath him.

"Darlin', I need to get off of you. We need to get you dressed and under the blankets to sleep." He hoisted himself up, watching her eyes staring at his cock. "Sorry. I'll be dressing over here."

He grabbed his pants and drawers off the floor and quickly dressed behind the privacy screen. By the time he came out, she'd put her chemise back on and lay under the blankets in bed, just as he'd asked her to.

"Good girl." He went over to her, tucking the blanket around her, kissing her forehead. "It's been a rough day, but it'll be over tomorrow. I'll stay and watch over you." He pointed a finger at her in warning. "But you stay in bed!"

"I will, Sir. I'm not leaving. You've saved me." The trust in her eyes went right to his core. He wasn't sure he deserved that kind of trust, not after the day they'd had together.

"Sleep well, Minnie."

He sat in the chair, watching her fall asleep, her chest hitching every now and then from all the tears she'd cried during her spanking — doubtless what she feared would be her defilement. He found himself wishing he had just a couple more days with her. It would be hard to drop her off to Angus and the Widow Wagon, to see her be married off to someone else. Someone who couldn't protect her like he could.

How had this slip of a woman stolen a part of his heart already? It didn't make sense. He needed to focus on getting these men arrested, and Minnie to safety. He'd worry about the rest later.

CHAPTER NINETEEN

"**A**ngus, you gotta wake up!" He couldn't open his eyes, let alone comprehend where he was or who was shouting his name.

"Angus! Get up! A telegram came about Minnie!"

Shit! It was Sam shouting through the tent door. Angus threw his pants on and didn't even put a shirt on before opening the flap. Clara had thrown a shawl over her shoulders, following right behind him.

"They've heard something?" Angus didn't dare to believe it. He'd increasingly feared they'd never get her back.

Sam was out of breath. "Yeah, the Sheriff just came by and told me to alert you. They said that they are in Independence Rock. He's gathering the men and they're going out there with the U.S. Marshals to rescue her and arrest the outlaws."

"How? Does anyone know details?" Clara had retrieved his shirt and boots, motioning Sam to come in so he could finish getting dressed.

"Nah. No one seems to know. They received a telegram from a U.S. Marshal out there who says they're in a saloon out there. They plan on raiding the place before sunrise. So we gotta get over to the Sheriff."

Angus jumped up, grabbing Clara, then Sam, hugging them both. "I'm so damn happy about this. I didn't think we'd ever get that sassy brat back. Damn, it'll be good to see her."

"That it will, Angus." Sam beamed back at him. They'd never lost a woman or child on the Widow Wagon, and if Angus had anything to do with it, they never would either. "I already took the liberty of talking to the people traveling with the Anderson wagon and asked if Tiny would be willing to watch our women until we can come back with Minnie. He said he'd be more than happy to."

"Jesus, thank you, Sam." Angus put his gun belt on and snatched up his rifle, pulling Clara close. "You behave! I'll be back with Miss Minnie, then we'll make our way to Idaho. Tell the women we'll be back by tonight. If not, we'll send word, and we will arrive by tomorrow morning."

"Lord, Angus, I'm not *five*. I know how to behave while you're gone." She rolled her eyes at Sam. "The women and I will be fine with Tiny and his wagon. Be safe, and tell Minnie I'm sorry about the fight and that I'm glad she's coming back."

"I'll do just that, darlin'. After I paint her ass as red as a barn door."

Clara swallowed. She knew he'd do just that once he knew she was safe.

He wouldn't be Angus if he didn't.

* * *

"Open the door, Red Clemmons! I know you're in there! Kane McKorrie, open up!"

The sound of feet running in the hall outside their room and the pounding of fists on the door had her waking out of her quiet slumber, Minnie bolted out of bed before even opening her eyes. "Sila—"

His hand clapped over her mouth, holding her back against his chest, his lips whispering at her ear. "Keep your mouth shut. Not a word. Are you going to listen and not speak?"

She nodded her head vigorously. He slowly took his hand off, and she turned to face him. He said in a low voice, "They're here to arrest them. They're going to tell them that we already left without them this morning. That way my cover won't be broken as a U.S. Marshal."

"Hey! Wait a damn minute!" Red shouted out in the hallway, over the sounds of a struggle. "Where the fuck is Silas? Are y'all arresting Silas too?"

The sheriff shouted, "Nope, heard from the innkeeper that he and the woman he was with left in the middle of the night." Their voices came closer to their door. "Looks like he abandoned you guys and went off to marry the girl."

She looked up at Silas and he waggled his eyebrows at her. "See, we done run off and got hitched."

She smiled at him, not sure what to say.

Kane shouted at Red. "Those sons-a-bitches! I *knew* we couldn't trust him, Red. I told you, and *told* you that something wasn't right about him. He took that woman and now we'll get nothing for her, but jail."

The Marshall shouted, "You men won't have to worry about any of this for a while. You'll be in jail or hanging soon. We've been hunting you down for years."

Finally, their heavy boots could be heard clomping down the stairs. Minnie held a hand to her chest. It was over. She'd made it — thanks to Silas — and she'd be fine.

167

"Minnie, where the hell are you?"

Angus!

She opened her mouth. "An—"

Silas slapped a hand over her mouth again, giving her backside a swat so hard that she shouted under his hand.

Jesus, my ass will never heal with this man around!

"I told you to keep your mouth shut. Do you ever follow directions, or do you need to feel the heat of a strap or switch every hour of the day to get it through to you?" He frog walked her to the privacy screen, taking his hand away from her mouth. "Stay put." He wagged a finger in her face. "Don't move. Don't say a word!"

He stomped to the door, opening it and leaning into the hallway. "Sir, can I help you? Are you looking for someone?"

She heard Angus walk up to the door. "I'm here to rescue someone who was stolen from those two renegades the Sheriff just arrested. Minnie Johnson? Have you heard of her since your stay here?"

"Well, that depends on who's asking. Who are you, sir?"

"I'm the wagon master for the Widow Wagon. Miss Minnie was kidnapped by those outlaws and we've been worried sick about her. As wagon master, I sure would like to get her back to safety if you know where she is." The strain in Angus' voice made tears spring to her eyes. He *cared*. She wasn't sure he'd care whether or not she ever came back.

"It's good to make your acquaintance, sir. The name is Silas Stone, U.S. Marshal. I can—"

She bounded out from around the privacy screen, bolting for the doorway. "Angus!" She threw herself into his arms. "I missed you. Oh, God! I've never been so happy to see you."

"Jesus, you're a sight for sore eyes. I thought we'd lost you!"

Silas yanked them both roughly into the room,

slamming the door behind them. He glared at Minnie. "I told you to stay put behind that privacy screen, and to keep your mouth shut! Damn you!"

Angus put his hands on his hips. "I see some things never change. Since you already have a reckoning from me, I'll just add Silas' reckoning to it too."

Silas looked at the wagon master. "I think—"

Angus cut him off with the wave of a hand, hauling Minnie roughly over his lap.

"Angus! Don't please, I don't think I can be spanked again." Her ass had been through so much in twenty-four hours, and she knew the gruff man didn't go in for half measures.

He lifted her skirts up, pulling her pantaloons over her bottom and whistling loudly. "What the hell happened here?"

"Well, sir, she had tried to—" Silas started to defend himself, his hesitancy plain — something she'd never heard in his voice before. Was it remorse? Guilt?

Minnie spoke then, knowing it would be better for Angus to hear it from her mouth. "Angus, I kind of asked for all of this. I was trying to escape and I bit Silas in the leg so hard that I tasted blood — and then ran into the desert to try to get away."

She looked over her shoulder to see the shock on Angus' face. He glanced at Silas for confirmation.

"I can show you, sir," Silas said. "I'll have a scar for the rest of my life. I've been putting ointment and alcohol on it several times a day to keep it from festering."

"No need. I have no doubt if you're both sayin' it." He helped Minnie to stand. "Keep your skirts up. Continue."

She shuffled her feet, knowing that her backside was facing Silas with her drawers at her ankles. She made sure her skirts drooped in front to hide her sex from Angus though. "And then I wanted to escape before I'd be forced to sleep with him. I didn't know who he was, Angus. I tried to escape, and I ran from the room in just my chemise down the stairs into the saloon area." She stared at the floor in front of her, too embarrassed to look Angus in the eye.

"Good God, woman. Do you have any idea what could've happen to you in a room full of drunken saloon men?" He shook his head. "It looks like Silas here knows how to tan a backside, I got to say. But how in the name of hell did you decide, with an ass that already looks like that, to *still* disobey him?"

"I don't know." She glanced over her shoulder at Silas who smiled at her. "I guess, I just didn't think. I was just so happy to see you." She reached out, grabbing Angus's hand.

Angus smiled up at her, then looked around her at Silas. "Marshal, I think you and I need to talk."

"Sir, before you even say it, let me speak. Minnie didn't know I was a marshal. She didn't know I was going to keep her safe, all of these incidents were to keep her safe and I needed her to fear me enough to listen. And I know that she's been compromised by me paddling her bare bottom. I swear I didn't take her sexually, but either way, she's been compromised."

He walked up to Minnie, taking her hands into each of his. She wondered if she was in trouble again. Between Angus and Silas, a girl didn't feel like her backside was ever safe. "Minnie, I know you were supposed to meet your mail order husband in Idaho, but if you'll take me, I would like to be your husband and have you live here in Wyoming."

She stared back at him. He'd kidnapped her, belted her, paddled her, laid with her as a man does with a woman — yet without violating her. He'd also protected her from Red and Kane. He'd stayed up all night to keep her safe. He'd gotten the renegades arrested, reunited her with Angus, and very likely saved her life. But she didn't know him — at all. She didn't know Tom Ferris, her soon-to-be mail order husband either. The truth was, she knew Silas much better than Tom Ferris, regardless of what had happened between them.

"You did your best to protect me — even from myself. And I don't know you very well, at all. Would we have to marry right off?" She bit her lip, wondering if she was pushing too far. But she wanted to be sure that he wasn't...mean. She wanted to be sure that he would treat her right.

"We have several days travel to get to my home in Green River. You can watch me and see if this is what you really want. If you don't, I'll bring you to meet Tom Ferris in Idaho. You have my word on that, Minnie."

Angus cleared his throat. "If it makes either of you feel better, we'll be traveling most of that way. At least to Sublette Cutoff. He can ride along with us and then you'll feel safe and I can rest assured that you're safe too."

Minnie stared into those deep green eyes and knew she'd take a leap of faith. "Yes, I'll take a chance and see if this is for us."

He pulled her in for a hug. "You won't be sorry, Minnie. I'm a good man. You'll see." And then holding her hand, he pulled her over to the bed, sitting down and tossing her over his lap. "And I regret to say that the next task falls to me rather than Angus. You have a habit of disobeying his rules for the Widow Wagon. Your poor little bottom is very sore, so it won't be a long spanking. But it will be memorable, I'm sure."

"Silas! No!" She didn't know where the energy came from, but she'd be damned if he laid another hand on her buttocks. She rocked and kicked, flailing her legs and arms, screeching and yelling. To no avail, of course. He rucked up her skirts, yanking on her drawers so hard she heard fabric rip. "You will stop this feral temper tantrum, now!"

His hand smacked the crest of her bottom so hard that she rocked forward on his lap, grasping his ankle for balance. His hand began to rain down slaps, hitting every stripe and bruise already decorating her poor hind end.

Desperate situations called for desperate measures though, and she dug her nails into his leg.

"Minnie! Drop your hand immediately or I'll grab my belt. Are you missing the sting of the leather this soon?"

He held her tightly with one hand while the other unbuckled it, the jingle of the tooth on the metal buckle was like an electric shock to her system.

She stilled, her ass and legs tingling in response to the sound. "No, no, oh please no! No, no, Silas!"

"That's what I thought. You're a smart girl, Minnie. But we'll keep it unbuckled just in case." He pulled her into his hip again, resuming her spanking, his hand punishing her fast and hard. Her legs stiffened straight behind her and she blubbered like an eight-year-old. She couldn't remember the last time she cried so hard — well, at least not since yesterday in the desert.

The punishment didn't last long and soon his hand stilled, though her sobs continued to rack her body. She felt so exhausted. For the third time in twenty-four hours, she promised herself that she'd listen to every single order that Silas uttered.

"I'm very impressed, Silas. That is a tough woman you're taking on — but you seem to know that already. I have to say, you seem to have a really good handle on how to apply discipline — consistently and firmly." Angus came over, clapping Silas on the shoulder. "Good man."

Minnie glared at him.

Who's side is he fucking on anyway?

Smack! "You will not glare at him," Silas barked. "You just received a spanking for not obeying him. He needs your respect. This man just delayed his wagon for you and came in the middle of the night to rescue you. Apologize now, or you'll stand in the corner with your red tail exposed until you're properly humbled."

Silas definitely wasn't the type of man to budge an inch. She'd have to figure this out quick, or she'd never be riding horses or wagons again.

"I'm sorry, Angus. Really, sorry." Looking up, she saw him smiling at her.

"I have no doubt that you're sorry, girl. I have a feeling you'll be in a sorry state for a while too." He chuckled, walking toward the door. "You two settle things here. I'll be downstairs at the restaurant for some breakfast, and then we'll make our way to the Widow Wagon."

CHAPTER TWENTY

Minnie sat with her arms crossed in front of her. She wasn't happy with either of the men she'd been forced to travel with back to the Widow Wagon. She stepped out into the bright sunlight in front of the hotel, only to find Silas patting a pillow laid across his lap and the saddle horn. She was touched that he'd made such an effort, trying to find a way for her to ride on her spanked bottom in some sort of comfort. Minnie certainly wasn't going to let him know that though.

"You must be a diagnosed idiot if you think I'm sitting on that pillow all the way to Devil's Gate. I might as well wear a sign that says, 'Yes, he paddled my ass raw. Thank you for asking.'"

She stood with her arms crossed. She'd simply refuse to leave until it was gone. Several passersby had gathered watching once they heard her voice raised in anger and the pillow sitting on the saddle horn. Their laughter and snickering could be heard behind her.

"Wilhelmina Louise! You're riding this horse. You'll be sick if you have to lie over my lap the whole way."

"Wait! Who told you my name?"

She shot an accusing glare at Angus, who held his

hands up in surrender. "He forced me to. I had no choice."

"I bet." She glared back at Silas. "I'm not sitting on a pillow. Everyone will know why I'm on it."

She heard the laughter of some small boys and grown men behind her. She swiveled on her heels, marching toward them. "I suggest you all find something to do besides listening in on others' conversations!" They all scattered, obviously seeing the rage in her eyes.

"If you don't straighten up your attitude, Miss Johnson, you're going to find your little backside being paddled with my riding crop here in front of the whole town." Silas fingered the end of the crop and then swished in the air next to him. The ensuing whistle made her shiver a little. It wouldn't be worth it. She'd toss the pillow out along the trail at some point. She'd just ride along until she could have her way.

Angus chuckled as she stomped her way over to Silas. "That is one cantankerous woman, Silas. Are you sure you know what you're signing up for?"

Silas picked her up as if she was a small child, placing her softly on the pillow, adjusting it until he was satisfied that she was comfortable. "Oh, she's not cantankerous at all, Angus. She's quite malleable once she knows who's in charge. She just hasn't met someone as stubborn as she is."

"Oh, I beg to differ. I'm as stubborn as she is. Ask my wife."

"Of that, I have no doubt. She'll learn though. I have a lifetime of spanking that gorgeous plump ass until it sashays and sways to the beat of my drum." He patted her bottom. "Isn't that right, Miss Johnson? Or should I say soon-to-be Mrs. Stone?"

"We'll see. I may change my mind."

He lightly kissed her temple. "You may, but I sincerely doubt it. I'm pretty charming when I want to be."

She snorted, muttering, "Aren't you all?"

They both laughed at her, and they started their journey to Devil's Gate. They'd be there by sundown.

* * *

She'd fallen asleep, leaning back on his chest. He couldn't imagine a better feeling in the world. Her slow, steady breathing relaxed him, the burdens of the day melting away. Minnie had been through a lot in the last day and a half, and he avoided jostling her as he could. He still felt bad for how her bottom looked, but he'd never seen such a stubborn woman in all his days. And when Angus told him that they'd dropped off a woman whose personality overshadowed the strength of Minnie's for weeks, he shook his head in amazement. The wagon master needed an award — or sainthood.

Feeling the press of her soft buttocks on his stiff cock didn't make the ride any more enjoyable for him either. He remembered the feel of her slight body under him, even though he didn't get to experience her completely. He remembered the warmth of her and the press of those pointed nipples against his chest and the thought had him as hard as he had been the night he'd lain with her. His penis had brushed against her moist pussy and he'd been barely able to restrain himself from pounding into her, thrusting into her slick juices. In spite of the obvious danger she'd been in, she'd been excited, her quim drenched with her excess.

He had to make her his wife. He'd been wanting a family, been more than ready for a while. His highly educated, cultured mother would be more than pleased with Minnie. He chuckled, thinking of how his father would enjoy her sassy mouth and ability to rile his normally calm and cool exterior.

Angus spoke, breaking Silas' thoughts away from sexual relations with his future wife. "So I need to ask you, while she's sleeping. What did she mean that you laid with her 'like a man does with a woman, but didn't violate her?'"

Silas took a deep breath, letting it out slowly. This wouldn't be easy. "Well, sir, to protect her, I told Red and Kane that she was mine. That, as she'd tell you, I'd be 'fucking her' that night. They knew and they expected it.

177

From past experiences that those two have had, they knew to listen for screams and cries, and I also knew from being with them for a while that they wouldn't hesitate to sneak a peek through a window or door to see if we were actually naked in bed."

He stopped stroking her hair off her face, giving her temple a soft kiss. "So, after she tried to escape, running into the saloon dressed in only her chemise, and giving me a heart attack."

"I bet. I almost had a heart attack hearing about it today. Christ, she really could've been hurt by any of those men in the saloon."

"So, you understand how the fear made me paddle her bottom? In hindsight, I probably should've waited a day or two after the strapping she'd received for biting me."

"Oh, hell, Silas, don't beat yourself up over that." Angus dismissed him with a wave of his hand. "I would've done the same. She deserved it for putting herself at risk."

"I know, but Christ it bothers me to see her little ass so bruised. I don't want her to feel bad and in pain, at my hand. I'm gonna have to learn how to discipline her in a more measured way, because apparently she can't go more than a few hours without tangling with someone."

"I can attest to that. I truly don't know how she held it together until Daisy left. But Daisy was like five hellcats put together. Her poor husband, Noah, must go to bed at night dead tired."

They both laughed, shaking their heads, just imagining how awful it would be. "Anyway, after I paddled the hell out of her ass, I told her it was time to do the next task of the evening. I stripped, and laid on top of her, but I swear I didn't penetrate or even come close to taking her." He stroked his hands over her arms, pulling her closer to him. "I immediately put my hand over her mouth and whispered that I was a U.S. Marshal and that we needed to do this in case Red and Kane were watching. I promised her that I was there to protect her and that I'd get her back to the Widow Wagon. As soon as she calmed down, I got off her, we got dressed; and I sat watching her sleep the rest of the night until y'all came to arrest them."

"God, that had to have been hard — for both of you. She must've been scared witless, and yet, you had to feel like the criminals you arrest." Angus pushed the brim of his hat up, wiping the sweat from his brow. "But I sure thank you for saving her. She may be some trouble, but she's a good girl. She'll make you a good wife. Trust me."

"Are you ready to shoot me or make a gunshot wedding?" Silas had no idea how Angus would respond. He was ready for any reaction at that point.

"Nah, Silas. You're of good stock. Anyone who'd go to the trouble you did to save a woman, and yet keep her from being defiled, is a good man. I ain't going to attack you." Angus stared at Minnie quietly for a moment. "And if I was a betting man — which I am sometimes — I'd say you two will be married within the month."

"From your lips to God's ears, Angus. I don't even understand it, but I can't imagine not having her in my life. How does that happen?" He was serious. He had not a clue how he'd fallen for a woman that quickly. He'd had women who'd thrown themselves shamelessly at him, but he'd never felt a thing for them. This slight, delicate woman with a naughty, fiery spirit had stolen his heart in less than twenty-four hours.

"Sometimes there's a thing called God's will, and no matter what, things fall into place at the right time. I've seen it many times in others' lives — and in my own."

They nodded at each other and continued their journey in silence. No additional words were necessary.

* * *

Minnie had been more than ready to make it to Devil's Gate. Even though it hadn't been a long ride, with a bottom as sore as hers, it felt much longer than it had actually been. And even though she'd been as mad as a wet hen at him for making her sit on that pillow, she would have never made it without the pillow.

When they pulled up to the wagon camp, the women of the Widow Wagon came out to them, screaming, shouting and crying. She struggled to get off the horse, and Silas laughed, helping her down before she hurt herself.

The four women — Margie, Lizzie, Minnie, and Clara stood in a huddle, just weeping. Minnie found it remarkable to feel such love from women who'd been complete strangers just a little over two months ago. And yet, these women who she'd slighted and fought with had forgiven her and taken her in as one of their own. It was more than humbling.

"Clara, Lizzie, Margie, I'm so sorry for the trouble I caused. I've been foolish and selfish. I promise that we'll move forward from this and you'll see I'm a changed person." Minnie had a hard time saying it through her tears, but she hoped that they knew she meant every word.

Clara threw her arms around Minnie's neck. "I swear I would never have forgiven myself if something happened to you on that trail. I felt so responsible for letting you go. Please forgive me."

At that point, Angus and Silas walked up to them, the wagon master speaking first. "We need to just let the past be the past. Mistakes were made all around, but it ended well and Minnie is back." He leaned back pulling Silas forward. "This gentleman here is Silas Stone. He's a U.S. Marshal — and was one of Minnie's renegade captors. He kept her safe, and is solely responsible for the arrest of the outlaws. He and Minnie have decided to travel with us to South Pass to determine if they are going to be married. I want you all to say hello and treat him with the respect he deserves."

"Angus, none of this is necessary, but thank you." Silas wrapped his arm around Minnie. "How could I not save a sweet woman like this?" He brushed the back of his knuckles on the side of her face, tucking a strand of hair behind her ear.

Everyone stood in silence observing them. Minnie looked up, realizing that they were all teary-eyed, staring at how Silas felt about her.

Angus clapped his hands together. "Okay, let's get us some grub. We're hungry. And as I said before, it's time for every one of you to cinch your saddle, and move forward."

The women scattered to cook the food for everyone, leaving Silas and Minnie standing arm-in-arm. "You think you might be happy with having a renegade in your life?"

"I like the thought of being your captive more."

Silas raised his eyebrows at her, giving her a slow, gentle kiss. "Let's see where this journey brings us, Miss Minnie."

ABOUT THE AUTHOR

Megan Michaels writes BDSM Erotic Romance that is either Contemporary or Western Historical. Her books delve into Domestic Discipline, Dominance/submission, and all of them have elements of BDSM. Megan Michaels' books are a sensual exploration into erotic romance. She loves a strong, alpha male who spanks, and if that man is a Dom or a cowboy...well then the perfect situation has been created.

Made in the USA
Coppell, TX
06 July 2020